#NotReadyToDie

#NotReadyToDie

Cate Carlyle

COMMON DEER PRESS

Published by Common Deer Press Inc.

© 2019 Cate Carlyle

David Moratto, cover and interior design

Published in 2019 by Common Deer Press
3203 - 1 Scott Street
Toronto, Ontario
M5E 1A1

Printed in Canada

Library of Congress Cataloging-in-Publication Data
Carlyle, Cate. - First Edition
#NotReadyToDie/Cate Carlyle
ISBN: 978-1-988761-39-8 (print)
ISBN: 978-1-988761-40-4 (e-book)

www.CommonDeerPress.com

Where you tend a rose my lad,
a thistle cannot grow.

—Frances Hodgson Burnett, *The Secret Garden*

Chapter 1

shifted my position, trying to stretch my stiff legs out a little bit while slowly and silently turning onto my back. I lifted both feet off the ground as I moved so my boots wouldn't drag on the floor and make a sound. No one could know we were inside. That's when I noticed the writing in green ink on the bottom of the desk. *Jarrod H. is a weiner 1981.* A wiener, really? Who would write that? Obviously someone less than stellar in the spelling department. And how would a student have had the opportunity to get under the desk to diss Jarrod in such a permanent way? Someone clearly felt strongly enough about him to take the time to vandalize school property in his honor. A jilted girlfriend? No, girls don't often use the term wiener. We're too mature. Wiener is a guy's word. And most girls wouldn't chance getting caught crawling under a desk to ink their feelings anyway. Too risky. Bathroom stalls all the way. In my experience, we tend to spread gossip and rumors when jilted, or cry into our pillows. Or maybe back in 1981 girls would've written nasty notes in the margins of their notebooks? We are typically much more passive aggressive with our disses, and sly, and smart. We are all about not getting caught and seeming like we couldn't care less anyways.

I wondered what had happened to Jarrod. Did he grow up to become an even bigger wiener and sire annoying little Jarrods? Or did he outgrow his wienerness, survive the bullying, and mature into a normal guy with a day job, a minivan, a wife and three kids, two cats, and a house with a huge mortgage?

Nowadays Jarrods are attacked online. A compromising Instagram pic or humiliating Snap—so many options. Phones across the school would ping as Jarrod's fate was sealed, all in seconds and all anonymous.

Whoever Jarrod was or is, and whoever had had a hate-on for him, they would never know how grateful I was for the few minutes of normalcy it gave me as I lay there pondering the vintage graffiti, Jarrod's fate, and why he was a wiener.

For those few peaceful moments, I wasn't thinking about the blood slowly seeping towards me from the desk in front of me. I had also succeeded in tuning out the incessant muffled whimpering coming from Mary Jane Schmidt. "MJ" was huddled under the desk beside me. She was one of those invisible kids, neither popular nor hated, neither weird nor cool, neither beautiful nor ugly. She wasn't in any cliques or sports clubs, and she got average grades. If she had gone off the deep end and committed a crime and I had been asked to describe her, I wouldn't have been able to offer anything. She was just *there*.

I tore my eyes away from the bottom of my desk and stretched my left leg out as far as I could to nudge MJ with the toe of my Blundstone. She jolted and looked over at me, her eyes glistening saucers and her hand clamped over her mouth and nose.

"Sshhh!" I mouthed, librarian style, with my index finger held up in front of my face.

MJ let out one last whimper then rested her head back on the dirty gray vinyl floor. She was probably in shock, as I'm sure many of my other classmates in Grade 11 Homeroom A were. Even during the practice lockdown we had all endured back in September it had been impossible to keep everyone quiet. And some classmates had reacted to the drill with instant panic, either babbling nonsense or blurting "We are all going to die!"

over and over like a mantra of doom. I knew that day that if we ever had a real emergency at school, an emergency that required silence, we would fail miserably. Some people rise to challenges in extraordinary circumstances, some crumble and collapse. MJ was clearly a crumbler, and the jury was still out on which category I fell into.

My mom always said I was strong like her grandma, my great grandma Gwyneth, a Holocaust survivor. I didn't think I was strong. Although maybe if I survived this day, I would be slightly worthier of comparison to Mom's "Gwynnie."

I glanced down at my phone, my lifeline to the outside world. It had been a gift from my dad, a unique model from Japan that a client had given him. Mom still hadn't answered any of my texts. She must have been busy at her library branch; she loved to brag that it was "the busiest and coolest hangout this side of Toronto." Mondays were usually quite hectic for her with returns from the weekend and toddler story times. Any other day of the week I knew she would have answered quickly, but still no reply to the text I had sent at 9:05 a.m.:

Gunshots in hall

I texted her again at 9:06:

Locked in homeroom

Then again at 9:08 as I remembered our fight that morning before school and felt bad for my earlier bitchiness and the bluntness of my first two texts:

ILY to infinity, Mom. SRY for this morning ♥

Don't worry!!!!!!! TTYS

Telling Mom not to worry was like telling the Kardashians to stop with the selfies. Not gonna happen. Since Dad's heart attack, Mom had glommed onto me and started an awkward ritual she insisted we do before we went to bed each night. Mom would say, "Love you to infinity, Gin," we'd fist bump, and then we'd both strike a superhero pose, chests puffed out, and hands on hips. Yes, I was named after Ginerva "Ginny" Weasley, the burden of being born to a librarian and an editor. It was a cross I had to bear. But, glass half full kinda gal that I am, I was pretty grateful to have not ended up a Matilda, or a Ramona, or a Scout. Mom and I had been fist bumping and posing for 945 days now. It was super dorky, and I'd die a thousand deaths if my friends ever saw me doing it, but if it helped Mom deal with her loss, then I'd suck it up. Always made me laugh at least.

I noticed a change in the noise in the room. MJ had gone silent. Had she passed out from the shock or finally calmed down? Either way, a good thing. I eased my leg back and away from her and made another attempt to get comfortable under my desk. If we were in this for the long haul, I'd need to figure out a better position. As I checked for the third time that my phone was on silent and went to tuck it back into the front pocket of my jeans, I noticed the battery icon had grown smaller. No one else had a charger for my model and my cord was sitting on my nightstand at home. My breath caught in my throat as I was reminded that my lifeline to normalcy was finite and the minutes were ticking down.

News Talk Radio 956
@NEWSTALK956

#BREAKINGNEWS: Reports of shots fired at local high school. Stay tuned. #education

9:12 AM–April 28, 2019. News Talk Radio 956
💬 250   ↻ 308   ♡ 201

Chapter 2

Weekday mornings at the Bartholomew house were always the same. So much the same that I once suspected that maybe I was an unwitting participant in a *Truman Show*-style experiment wherein nothing changed and I was living under a dome and being watched for others' entertainment. Mom, the person responsible for my obsession with 80s and 90s pop culture, assured me we weren't being watched and that I wasn't that entertaining. Susan Bartholomew, Mom, was a morning person, always awake by 6am without an alarm and happier than anyone should be at that God-awful time of day. I, on the other hand, was a night owl. While Mom was tucked in bed with a book by 9:00 every weeknight (10:30 on weekends when she was really letting her freak flag fly), I was usually up until 1 or 2 a.m.. I wrote my best papers after 11 p.m., sent witty texts to my besties, and I finally made it to the bottom level of the mine in *Stardew Valley* after midnight. My brain never truly woke up until the sun went down. Most of my friends were also up super late and we chatted and Snapped online until the wee hours.

Unfortunately, my vampire-like existence turned Mom's 6:00 a.m. wake-up call into my own private hell. I always set the alarm on my dad's old-school clock radio, and I set my phone alarm with the volume on max, and Mom would also try her best to wake me when I hit the snooze button a few too many times.

She'd nudge me at 6:00 a.m., then again at 6:15, then again at 6:30. By 7:00 a.m. she'd usually push me until I fell off the side of my bed. I would then wander trance-like into my bathroom to submit myself to the jarring effects of a cold shower. By the time I was dry and dressed, hair braided, blush and eyeliner applied, and sitting at the kitchen island with a cup of Mom's masala chai tea in hand, I was a bit more capable of carrying on a conversation and at least appearing to be fully awake.

This particular Monday morning was different. Mom and I had done the wake-up dance, I had showered, and I was seated at our long butcher block island by 7:30 a.m., but not with tea in hand. Mom had run out of chai and she was running late. That *never* happened. Mom was as punctual as a drill sergeant and our chai tea stash could keep all of India quenched for at least a year. This Monday morning, Mom was running around the L-shaped kitchen, gathering a makeshift lunch of Mr. Noodles, a banana, and packaged applesauce and frantically trying to find her favorite silver charm bracelet, the one Dad had gifted her for their 20th anniversary. The bracelet featured a charm for every year they were married, including a little book, a letter G, a heart, and a lighthouse. All held special meaning for Mom and Dad.

"I can't find it anywhere, Gin Gin. I'll never forgive myself if I've lost it. Where could it be?!"

"I am sure you haven't lost it, Mom. You know how you're starting to forget things in your twilight years; maybe you left it at work?"

Mom looked me in the eyes and then, with a half-smile, she reached over and pushed the sleeve of my hoodie up on my right arm.

"You've borrowed it to impress that cutie pie Owen haven't—"

The words caught in her throat as she took in the red gashes crisscrossing my forearm just below the elbow. She gasped and her hand flew to her mouth just as my hand flew to my sleeve, yanking it back down to conceal the angry maze of scars.

"You're cutting again, Gin Gin!" she screeched before launching into a string of comments I'd heard several times before. "Why didn't you tell me, or ask for help? You know you can talk to me. We can find you a counselor again. Oh Ginny. What would your father think, you hurting yourself like this? Are you trying to kill yourself? I wouldn't survive if I lost you too!"

I tuned Mom out and let her babbling fade to white noise. How could I explain so that she would understand? How could I describe the euphoric feeling when the scissor blade touched my flesh and I could finally feel something, really *feel* something? She would never understand. Since Dad's death, there were weeks at a time when I felt nothing other than a dull numbness; the world swirled around me like a hurricane and I was stuck in the eye, merely existing. On the nights when I could hear her crying softly in her room the cuts brought me instant calm. The blood would bubble up and I could exhale. The hurt that rose up unexpectedly and unchecked when I would remember my dad and feel his absence, his aftershave wafting by on the bus or his favorite AC/DC song on the radio, it all seemed to go away after I cut. No, she wouldn't get it. We'd been through this before—the talks, counselors, and arm checks—in the months after Dad's death. She clearly knew nothing had changed and she still didn't understand it.

"God Mom, chill!"

She reddened, chastised, and let out a long breath.

"I know you worry Mom, and I know you care. Can we not do this right now?" I begged. "We're both late. How about you read me the riot act tonight instead, and you can remind me then how ungrateful and irresponsible I am?"

I regretted it the moment I said it. Mom looked at me with the saddest face, like a puppy kicked to the curb. She didn't deserve it. I was tired and missing Dad, and it was Monday. Sometimes I couldn't control what came out of my mouth.

"Fine, I will see you tonight and we will talk about this."

"Sure, whatever," I called back, grabbing my black pleather backpack and heading out the side door.

"I love you, sweetie. You know that, right?" she called after me. "Have a good day!"

I didn't turn or look back, I didn't tell her I loved her too, or give her a hug, or make a comment about how her hair looked particularly good today, curled away from her face. I didn't say or do anything.

My last words to my father had been, "See you tonight" as he'd headed off to the gym. He'd replied with an, "I love you, sweetheart," but I hadn't said anything else because I was too absorbed in a game on my phone.

It wasn't until a few hours later, huddled and shivering under my desk, that I realized my last words to my mother might forever be "Sure. Whatever."

John Thomas
@johnnybegood

Our school is under siege. In lockdown. Help us, we are terrified #surreal

9:22 AM–April 28, 2019. Southwestern High School
32 108 198

Chapter 3

Owen **Sanders always** took the desk in front of me in home-room. He invariably arrived late to school and would race in after the bell, skidding into his chair like he was taking home plate. He'd turn back around to me with his huge Cheshire Cat grin.

"Made it just in time, Ginny! Miss me, sweet thing?"

"Nope, Owen. Didn't even notice you weren't here."

Same banter every morning. But not today.

I lifted my neck up off the floor so I could see Owen better. He was curled in the fetal position, lying in a small pool of his own blood. He was covering his nose with one hand and a crimson tide was seeping out between his fingers. I assumed he had a bloody nose, maybe even broken, from banging his face on the corner of his desk as he scrambled to get under it. I waved my hand in the air in his direction to get his attention. Owen lifted his head slightly and looked at me with an expression I will never forget. I can only describe it as deflated. He looked as though all of the life had been sucked out of him, his face ghostly pale, dark rings around his eyes and tears streaming down. Not the usual happy-go-lucky, cheeky Owen, the guy who sang his way through the day deliberately off key and with the wrong lyrics, the guy who had never made an enemy, the Archie in our Riverdale (the old-school comic Archie, when Archie was a simple, innocent, freckled, standup guy, not the TV series.).

Today Owen looked terrified and in pain. I pointed to his nose and made a breaking-in-two gesture with my hands. Owen shook his head no and slowly stretched his right leg out straight. Blood was seeping from his jeans and I recognized it as the source of the rusty smell I had been breathing in. Owen had his other hand clamped high up on his thigh and he let go for a few quick seconds, revealing a hole in his jeans. It took me a moment to realize that the gleaming white object visible through the hole was probably Owen's bone. I gasped involuntarily, and searched Owen's eyes for any kind of explanation. He once again clamped his hand down over the hole in his leg, temporarily slowing the blood, and released his other hand from his nose. He made a gesture towards me as though he was holding an invisible gun and pulling the trigger. Owen had been shot.

News Talk Radio 956
@NEWSTALK956

#BREAKINGNEWS: Police and SWAT on scene. Parents alerted to shooter @SouthwesternHS. Stay tuned. #education

9:30 AM–April 28, 2019. News Talk Radio 956
♡ 202   ⟲ 489   ♡ 323

That morning Principal Herman (PeeWee to those who dared) had no sooner finished his morning announcements on the PA and signed off with his cringe worthy "There is no I in team, but there is an E for everyone," when what sounded like firecrackers or backfires erupted outside. But it wasn't a holiday and the parking lot was far enough away that backfires were unlikely too. I was seated at my usual desk waiting for the substitute, Miss Jones, to come in from the hallway. Mrs. Turner was our regular Homeroom A teacher, but she was out on maternity leave and not due back for another week, just in time to close out the last month of the school year. I leaned over my desk to peer out the windows but couldn't see any fireworks or cars billowing smoke. The rest of the class was chattering away, discussing their weekend and who had hooked up, or split up, or gotten wasted. Jace, Steve and, Gregg with two Gs, the Jocks, were droning on about how many goals and puck bunnies they'd scored; head cheerleader Conny and her crew of Barbies were reliving their cheer competition in mind numbing detail; the Tech Nerds were silent, necks craned, thumbs tapping away on their Switches. All of the seats were occupied, except for Owen's.

I looked around and noticed that Miss Jones was standing in the doorway. The door was closed half-way and she was frantically waving her arms and stage whispering, "Come on! Hurry! HURRY!"

Owen finally appeared, racing through the doorway as three more firecrackers went off.

POP!

POP!

POP!

Miss Jones disappeared outside into the hallway for a split second as the piercing wail of the school's fire alarm sounded. She then reappeared in the doorway, bent over double and made an odd grunting noise as though someone had kicked her in the gut and knocked the wind out of her. She grabbed her belly as she frantically rushed back into the room, slamming the door shut behind her. She locked the deadbolt, slammed all four light switches down with one swift flick of her wrist, pulled down the half blind covering the window at the top of the door, and then slid the bolt above the handle across until it was showing a blue bar. The blue bar was a signal for those outside that all assigned students were locked in the classroom. No one was missing.

Miss Jones raced to the opposite side of the room and yanked down the window blinds at hyper speed while whispering, "Under your desks! Now! Not a drill! Under your desks! Now! This is not a drill!" Easy going, soft spoken, crunchy granola Miss Jones had been replaced by this powerhouse on a mission to secure the room and get everyone hidden under their desks. I suddenly clued in that the alarm was not signaling a fire. Miss Jones was getting us out of the line of fire. Gunshots, not firecrackers.

Switching into autopilot, I followed Miss Jones's commands, clambered off my chair and curled up under my desk. A calm comes over me in a crisis, almost as if a robotic alien takes over my body and does what needs to be done. When my dad died, people worried I wasn't crying enough, or sleeping enough, or sad enough. I became this cool, numb automaton.

I noticed that not all of my classmates were following my

lead or Miss Jones's pleas. The Jocks were still standing huddled around Jace Goodwin their witless leader, captain of the football team, swim team, and hockey team. I was convinced that if Jace ever suffered a head injury, confetti would come flying out of his ears. Piñata Jace. The Jocks were completely ignoring Miss Jones and acting like alpha males showing the rest of us cowards who was really in charge. When Boot, their favorite punching bag, suddenly raced out of the class washroom and slid under the desk beside them at lightning speed two Jocks reached under, grabbed him by the scruff of the neck, and effortlessly hauled him back out.

"Where you going so fast, Boot Snack?"

"What you scared of?"

"Why don't you run out into the hall and see what's going on, BS?"

Poor Boot Snack would never live down the fact that on our third-grade camping trip he had stored teddy grahams in his shoes during morning hike. He would have been fine had he not let others see him pull out the sweaty snacks and savor them. To seal his fate, he then offered to share a few with the sporty boys/baby Jocks when they took notice. He had been branded "Boot Snack," BS for short—I wasn't sure which was worse—from that day on. One burden of small town life is attending elementary and high school with the same kids who knew your history and all of your secrets. No escape. I don't think anyone even remembered Boot's real name anymore. Arturo? Othello? Something weird like that, if I recall. Maybe he preferred BS? I doubt it.

I was watching Miss Jones's face as she noticed that the huddle of Jocks was ignoring her, all still standing and talking and not even thinking of getting under their desks. I saw her slowly transform from meek teacher to rabid she-wolf.

"Get under your desks, NOW students! Please, you MUST! For all our sakes. You know what to do in lockdown. We've practiced this. I know you can do this! Unfortunately, this is not a drill, it is a matter of life and death," she whispered as loudly as she could. The veins in her neck were bulging out and her face had turned bright red as sweat droplets dripped down from her forehead. Those arrogant Jocks must have seen something in Miss Jones's face, a brewing combination of frustration, desperation, terror and anger, as they each finally attempted to curl their brawny man-child selves under the three by three foot desks.

With everyone on the floor, Miss Jones remained standing and scanned the room, double-checking with a silent headcount. Count complete, I watched her walk over to the door, lean back against it, close her eyes, and slide down to the floor like a snow-man melting. I could hear her ragged breaths as they rattled slowly out of her chest. The young substitute looked as though she had aged twenty years in the last five minutes, her face ashen and her mouth pinched, both arms wrapped around her torso.

"We can do this," she whispered, her voice getting weaker and weaker. "We can do this. We can do this together. Just stay under your desks and stay super quiet. I am so proud of all of you. I know you got this." Was she trying to convince herself or us?

Watching her fade, I finally clued in and realized that Miss Jones had been shot all while saving my Owen.

Sarah Somers
@butterflykisses

Girls' junior volleyball team all fine in Gym B for now. Shots going off. Get us out of here! #scared #loveyouall #prayforus #notreadytodie #thisiscanada #WTF

9:41 AM–April 28, 2019. Southwestern High School
♡ 67 ↻ 346 ♥ 113

A fter those initial few pops outside our classroom door, the school had gone eerily quiet. The fire alarm was a far-off droning backbeat now that the door was sealed, and the room was dim with the lights off and blinds closed. Whoever had been shooting in the hallway outside our door had moved on to another area, or was reloading, or was holed up somewhere biding their time for another attack. Some students had chosen to huddle in pairs under the desks, comforting each other, whimpering. Some pairs were simply friends drawn together in terror, and others were dating couples. The glow of phone screens flitted off and on like fireflies in the room as kids texted their parents or searched for news online of what was happening outside. When Gregg with two Gs' "Hotline Bling" ringtone suddenly sounded, jarring everyone as it broke the stillness, Miss Jones swiftly instructed that all phones must be on silent or turned off.

"Please guys, cells on silent. No one is going to die on my watch. I'll never get a full-time position if that happens."

She was obviously in pain, her voice barely above a whisper, scratchy and raw, yet Miss Jones was still trying to crack a joke. *Kudos, Miss Jones. I didn't know you had it in ya.*

The class seemed to finally be getting the message. Even the sound of my stomach growling seemed like a shout in the silence as I remembered I had not eaten or had my cup of tea that morning. I pushed my sleeve up and traced the scars on my forearm with my thumb. When I couldn't cut, the feel of the smooth raised edges would sometimes calm me and get me out of my head. But not this day. I noticed one of the K-something Barbies watching me (Keira? Kara?), one of the interchangeable pony-tailed blondes, and I quickly snapped my sleeve back in place. She raised a perfectly sculpted eyebrow at me.

As far as I knew, I had been genius at keeping my dirty little secret just that. But it seemed that the proverbial cat was clearly now out of the bag. If we survived this day, I would either have to own it or come up with a brilliant excuse for what she had seen. The Barbies had a gossip chain that could spread a rumor faster than one of Donald Trump's explosive tweets.

Though I tried not to do it too often, I could lie in a pinch. I could claim that the scars were from a particularly nasty run-in with a barbed wire fence. Or an athletic injury and resulting surgery that went wrong. But me and sports ... that would never fly. Or the result of an exploding glass Pyrex dish. That had actually happened to me. I'd go with that if need be. Or maybe I wouldn't have to explain? Who knew how this day would end up? Then again, my scars were probably the least of my worries considering I was trapped in lockdown with a gunman on the loose.

I checked my phone again. No reply from Mom. I looked over at Owen who was still curled in the fetal position, white as a sheet, clutching both his nose and his leg. I couldn't reconcile that sad lump with the Owen I knew. The Owen who didn't know that if he didn't ask me soon, then I was going to make the prom proposal. The Owen who didn't know that when we had played spin the bottle in fourth grade in my best friend's basement I had begged her to weigh the bottle so it was rigged and only I would get to kiss Owen (she did, but Owen got chicken pox and didn't show, and I got Jerkwad Jace who tried to cop a feel in lieu of a kiss). The Owen who didn't know that the golden flecks in his chestnut brown curls caught the morning sunlight and made me catch my breath each and every morning. The Owen who didn't know that I sent the "From your secret admirer XO" Valentine rose to him every year. The Owen who was oblivious to the fact that the best part of my day was when he texted me before going to bed each night, even though the text was always a friend zoned, "Sleep tight, good buddy (complete with poo emoji)!"

It may have been the sight of the drop of blood beading on one of Owen's curls that flipped the switch for me, but at that moment I decided that I was damned if I was going to let a homicidal predator destroy my Owen, or mess up my plans for prom, or force my Mom to host another funeral. Screw it! I couldn't take another minute curled under my desk, helpless, waiting for the worst to happen. If we were locked in this room for another ten hours or even another ten minutes, I was going to do what I could to make sure we all emerged alive. I couldn't just sit and wait while Owen bled out.

I remembered that when Mom had first caught me cutting she'd sent me to a therapist who had gone on and on about self-talk. I'd attended the required sessions, listened, promised to do the homework, and said what Dr. Lee wanted to hear: "I'm not cutting anymore ... When I get overwhelmed or anxious, I ask myself 'What's the worst that could happen?'. It's so helpful ... I tell myself to stop listening to the negative voices and focus on the positive ... I tell myself that the cuts are only masking my inner pain temporarily ... You are a genius, thank you so much for helping me Dr. Lee!"

I told my mom all about self-talk and how it had cured me, all lies, and proceeded to cut the bottoms of my feet where no one could see.

But things are different when you are desperate and there are no sharp objects around. With nothing to lose, I gave the self-talk a try and told myself that we would all get out alive and that if no one else was going to do something then it would have to be me. I even struck a superhero pose in my mind for Mom.

I slithered out from under my desk and looked around the room for anything I could use for reinforcements. I noted that the moveable three-panel whiteboard at the front of the classroom could serve as an extra barrier against any bullets that may come through the wall and into our group of sitting ducks. I crawled on all fours and tried to push the whiteboard over towards the inner wall while still staying down on my knees. The stupid thing was heavier and harder to push than it seemed. I could barely budge it on my own. I was looking back, hoping someone would see what I was trying to do and come help me, when suddenly the board started to move.

I fell forward as it left my hands. The petite perky Barbie who'd been spying on me, Kara or Keira or Kayla from the desk beside me, had come over to help and was pulling the other end. We slid it over and locked the wheels so that its 15-foot expanse served as an extra layer of protection from the shooter or shooters in the hallway. I tilted my head at Barbie in silent thank you and then gestured over towards the door and the crumpled Miss Jones. I raised my eyebrows and motioned to her to follow me so we could check on the teacher. We scooted down the board and were startled by what we discovered.

Miss Jones was keeled over sideways, clutching her stomach. Her eyes were closed and she was as still and pale as a porcelain doll. Barbie got to her before I did and grabbed Miss Jones's hand to check for a pulse, giving me a thumbs up and a brief smile when she found one. Miss Jones was alive, a small mercy.

Barbie motioned to me that we should drag Miss Jones back towards the windows and away from the hallway side of the room and she lifted her up under her armpits. I hoisted the teacher's limp legs and we awkwardly carry-dragged her, laying her down under the windows, a river of red trailing behind us. I then clambered over to Jace's desk and yanked his jean jacket down off of it while muttering "useless a-hole" under my breath.

While his classmates were bleeding out, or frozen in terror, or trying to save their teacher, big tough Jace was playing some pointless game on his cell and finishing off the last bite of a CLIF Bar. If we were in this for a long haul, I'd make sure Jace was the last one hauled out of this room.

I spread his extra-large stonewashed jacket over Miss Jones's legs, then grabbed someone's water bottle off the windowsill and held it to the teacher's mouth. Not the time to worry about germs or ownership. Miss Jones weakly parted her lips and took a drop or two of water like a baby bird before retreating back into herself. While I was trying to get the teacher to drink, Barbie had removed her own beautiful pink paisley scarf and was using it as a tourniquet around Miss Jones's middle to staunch the bleeding from her gunshot wound. The scarf seemed to be doing the trick. Silk? Those airhead cheerleaders had money and style. Barbie frowned up at me and shook her head no. It didn't look good for Miss Jones. We locked eyes for a moment and Barbie pulled her phone out of her pocket. She swiftly typed a note and passed the phone over to me.

Hemorrhagic shock
Weak pulse
Massive blood loss
Cold to touch
She needs a medic
Only one hit?

I processed what she had written, then typed back:

Owen Sanders was hit
He doesn't look good
Need to check on him too

It was only as we were crawling over towards Owen's desk that I realized that a Barbie had used a four-syllable word and, most likely, spelled it correctly. WTF? Also, I swear I saw Oompa Loompa wallpaper when Barbie opened her phone. The day could not get any more surreal ...

News Talk Radio 956
@NEWSTALK956

#BREAKINGNEWS: Operations ongoing. Believed one lone gunman. Parents gathering at scene. #education #staytuned #storydeveloping

10:01 AM–April 28, 2019. News Talk Radio 956
♡ **213** ↻ **501** ♡ **400**

Chapter 6

By the time Barbie and I got to Owen (mere seconds as we were quickly getting quite adept at silently crawling on all fours in and around the desks and chairs), he had turned a ghastly shade of gray. Nurse Barbie quickly, and expertly as far as I could tell, checked Owen's pulse on his wrist and then laid his arm back down. He seemed to be sleeping, and Barbie confirmed he was definitely still alive, giving me the thumbs up on the pulse.

Nurse Barbie then looked at his face and leg and then the dried pool of blood curving like a chalk outline around his body. I guessed that the lack of fresh liquid meant that the blood had been staunched, for now. I watched as she patted his shoulder gently and smoothed down some of the sticky blood covered curls behind his ears. She was definitely full of surprises, that one, with her medical terms and soothing bedside manner. It was probably all for show. *Trying to hone in on my Owen now, Barbie? Not gonna happen.* We both sat cross-legged on either side of Owen, catching our breath for a moment and taking in the enormity of the war zone that our classroom had become. Nurse Barbie caught my eye and leaned over towards me.

"Nice one back there with Jace. He is a total a-hole."

I nodded in agreement.

"We went out once and I've always regretted it."

I didn't say anything, caught off guard by her confession and unsure where it was going.

"We were playing pool in his basement after the date and then I woke up in his bedroom, wearing only his shirt, with no recollection of how I got there."

"Wow, Barb—er … that's brutal. I guess I underestimated his creepiness, if that's possible. Did you tell anyone?"

"No," she said, "you're the first. Figure someone should know in case I don't get out of here today. My grandma always said it's not good to die with untold stories. I was embarrassed and ashamed at the time. I couldn't remember anything so I thought no one would believe me. Thought it might become a he-said, she-said thing. I'm pretty sure he slipped something in my cola."

"Jeez, that's awful um …"

She pointed at her chest, "Kayla."

"I know," I lied.

She gave me a sad half-smile, "Right."

Kayla (after our pseudo-bonding moment I guessed I could try to stop calling her Barbie just for the day) fidgeted nervously with her rubber Southwestern Cheer bracelet for a minute then seemed to refocus and leaned back down towards Owen. She gently adjusted his legs so that his knees were bent a little bit more and tilted his head to the side.

"Recovery pose," she whispered. "I volunteer at the veterans' hospital after school."

I nodded like I knew that, or like I was also out there changing lives and helping people after school. I wasn't. Kayla was definitely not what I expected and I had a nagging suspicion I was only starting to scratch the surface with this girl. I hated to admit it, but her bedside manner was inspiring, while mine on the other hand, would best be described as non-existent. When I was little and stayed home sick from school, Dad was always the one who stayed home with me. He'd say that he was working his second job as Dr. Dad on those days. Dad would ask me where it hurt and no matter where I pointed his reply was always the same: "Oh no, doesn't look good. I am afraid that we will definitely have to ambertake."

I couldn't pronounce *amputate* as a child and it would forever be *ambertake* in our house, like *spaghetti* would always be *passgetti*, or like Sunday *roast beast*. The ambertake diagnosis never ceased to bring on a fit of giggles, with Dr. Dad chasing me around the house while I squealed with mock fear, "No ambertake, Dr. Dad! No ambertake!"

Dad would always catch me and fling me fireman-style over his shoulder. "Phew! Dr. Dad is so tired from chasing you, that there will be no ambertaking today."

Our ambertake chase always made me feel better, which I'm sure was his plan all along. On the day of his funeral, when Mom and I had one last moment alone with him before they lowered his casket, I kissed the lid and whispered, "I love you, Dr. Dad. I'm sorry I couldn't make you better."

Jeez Dad, I sure miss you

Lost in my memories it took me a moment to realize my phone was vibrating. I reached down and pulled it out of my pocket. Four texts from Heather, Mom's supervisor:

> **Ginny! Mom here. Are you okay???**
> **I love you!!!!!**
> **I missed your texts, forgot phone at home.**
> **A patron told me what's going on. Are you in a classroom??**
> **♥ Mom XOXOXOXO**

I texted back.

I'm fine
Lockdown in homeroom
Teacher and Owen were hit :(
WTF?

I waited anxiously while the ellipsis flashed showing me that Mom was typing. I had been able to hold it together and be relatively useful until that moment. Mom's texts made it more real somehow; I could feel her anxiety and her fear in those few lines. And, God love her, my mom would not text a contraction if it was her last day on earth. She texted like she was writing snail mail, punctuation and grammar on point, and each word tapped out at sloth speed, with one dainty finger. Mom used to address her texts "Dear Ginny:" 'til I gently let her know that only *older* people did that. The fastest way to get Mom to stop doing something was to tell her that it made her seem old.

The news says it is a shooter in the hall.
Maybe one of the staff??
He might even be holding someone hostage.
The police and SWAT team are outside.
Stay put and stay low!
I am on my way.
I LOVE YOU!!!!!!!!
♥ Mom XOXOXO

I texted Mom back:

Love you too
I'll be fine
TTYL XOXO

I turned my screen towards Kayla and shared the texts.

"I know," she whispered, "some of the news sites are starting to post about it now. Saying it's one of the night custodians, armed to the teeth and claiming to have bombs and grenades too."

"Jeez," I whispered, "we've become the daily news. You'd never think this'd happen here."

We both looked towards the door at that moment, neither speaking, letting it all sink in.

"Hey," Kayla whispered, "saw your arm earlier. What happened?"

The way Kayla said it, I figured that she knew the answer already or at least suspected as much. There was something in her tone and the knowing look she gave me.

"Oh that," I said laughing it off, "I'm a walking cliché I guess. A Netflix mini-series: Quirky girl's father, the sun in her world, dies suddenly, leaving girl to self-medicate with morose 90s playlists, a memorial tatt, and cutting until a hot newbie with tousled hair moves to town, falls in love with her, and fixes everything. Cue credits and Alanis Morissette's 'You Learn' — Oh, but my tale doesn't have a sexy outsider or a happy ending it seems."

"No seriously, Ginny. You okay? You want to talk about it?"

"I'm fine," I insisted, my standard response for everyone. "The cutting helps me cope sometimes. Hard to explain. It's not often; I can stop whenever I want to."

"If you say so. What's the tatt?"

I lifted up my pant leg to reveal the tiny Gryffindor House tattoo on the inside of my left ankle that I'd gotten the day after Dad died.

"My parents are both huge *Harry* fans," I explained.

"No duh," Kayla smiled.

Just then another shot went off, farther away. *POP!* Then two more. *POP! POP!* We both snapped our heads back at the sudden violent break in the silence. Then the fire alarm abruptly stopped its incessant wail. Our bonding moment screeched to a halt.

This was happening and it was real. I was locked in my classroom with a shooter on the loose in the halls. This was not a drill. I shuddered, closed my eyes, then heard a loud bang and all faded to black.

Mr. Gentleman
@Scienceguy

Class locked in. All accounted for. Stay safe.
Students, don't tweet your location!!

10:22 AM–April 28, 2019. Southwestern High School
♡ 75   ↻ 685   ♡ 412

Chapter 7

The summer I turned twelve years old Mom, Dad, and I went on a road trip to the East Coast. Dad's family, including his only sibling, Uncle Stew, all lived in Halifax. Uncle Stew had been fighting brain cancer for a few months. Stew's prognosis was not good and he had been given a few weeks to live. When Dad heard the news, he decided we should drive east to see my uncle during summer vacation. It took us two days to get there, Mom and Dad taking turns at the wheel while I was tucked in my nest of books, snacks, and blankets in the backseat. We played the license plate game, an essential part of any Bartholomew car trip. Dad always won with the longest list of different plates; he had an eagle eye and front seaters always had the advantage anyways. That road trip, we loaded up on one dollar gas station hot dogs with all the fixin's whenever we had to stop for bathroom breaks, we went through six boxes of Timbits on the twenty-hour drive, and I read four books, the entire Scott Westerfeld *Uglies* series. It was a great road trip, the three of us safe and together with no obligations or distractions and the bleak purpose of the journey shoved aside and unmentioned until we arrived.

Once we arrived in Halifax, we stayed at Uncle Stew's house for three days and didn't see my paternal grandparents at all while we were there. I often talked to Nonna and Poppa on the phone from Ontario, and they had been to visit at our house a few times on their way south to Florida in the winter, but we did not see them that week. While my parents never discussed or explained it, I somehow knew that my uncle and his parents did not speak. I'd heard rumblings over the years about the three of them, hushed chatter through my parents' bedroom walls.

"Your parents are such idiots, they aren't getting any younger and now that Stew's sick they are willing to lose him without ever reconnecting?" Mom had whispered.

"I know Susan, I've tried to talk to all three of them. Mom and Dad haven't spoken to Stew since he came out. They're a product of their time, I guess, and can't wrap their heads around Stew's sexuality."

"Well, they are a product of their own stupidity if you ask me. Don't make excuses for them, Stephen. How on earth did they ever end up with such great sons?"

I'd always known Uncle Stew was gay. I don't remember being told that he was or it ever needing any explanation, he just was. He was also the funniest, happiest, most handsome man I knew. He had piercing blue eyes, a lazy endearing drawl and an incredible mane of loose brown curls. He could cook like a professional chef, was the top golfer at his favorite Cape Breton club, and drove a V-Rex motorbike like in *The Fast and the Furious*. He called it his baby.

But when we visited that summer, that man was nowhere to be seen. The shabby chic front room of Uncle Stew's downtown walk-up, which had been professionally decorated with vintage finds, contemporary art, and imported rugs, had been transformed into a makeshift hospital room complete with adjustable bed, oxygen tank, and all the bells and whistles associated with dying. Uncle Stew had around-the-clock care and a constant stream of friends and colleagues visiting him, bringing his favorite take out dishes and refreshing the opulent floral bouquets scattered throughout his house. My Uncle Stew, the Uncle Stew I knew and loved, had already left the building. In his place was a lifeless bald man in a hospital bed who we talked to while he slept all day and night, whose every breath was a struggle, and who gave off an odor reminiscent of museums or long-sealed linen closets.

Mom and Dad helped to change and bathe Uncle Stew. They read to him and kept up a constant stream of chatter about old times and memories. I stayed on the periphery, trying to keep my tears from escaping, and was amazed at how everyone was acting as though Uncle Stew was still somewhere in that shriveled husk.

The day before we left Nova Scotia, four days before Uncle Stew finally let go, Dad took me out to see the Peggy's Cove lighthouse. He told me that it was an iconic national symbol and a must-see when in the Maritimes. We drove the twisty roads for about thirty minutes, taking us out of the city, and marveled at how the landscape turned from green-treed boulevards to an odd lunar landscape complete with giant boulders seemingly dropped from the sky at random. Dad and I each had the local specialty, Moose Tracks waffle cones, in the Peggy's Cove tourist shop while we waited for the fog to lift. We then walked out to the lighthouse, always careful to stay on the dry rocks and avoid the wet black ones that could become submerged by a rogue wave at any moment.

"I'm glad you came, Ginny," he said. "I know it wasn't easy for you."

"It's fine, Dad. I know I wasn't much help, but I kinda felt like that person wasn't Uncle Stew anymore, you know?"

"I know. And you're right, it's best to remember the Uncle Stew we knew and loved. The guy who loved life and lived every minute of it."

I noticed a tear trickling down Dad's cheek and wiped it away for him.

"Thanks, Gin Gin," he sniffled. "Can you do me a favor?"

"Anything, Dad," I said.

"Ok, dad-speech alert, my dear girl. Life is awesome and incredible and so damn short. Don't waste a day. Sure, it can be tough and frustrating, and we don't always get what we want, but there are so many amazing places to see and people to love and new things to try. I am proud of you no matter what, but I wouldn't be fulfilling my dad duty if I didn't tell you how quickly it all goes by and how you have to make the most of each and every second."

It was my turn to start tearing up. I swiped a few tears off my cheeks and mumbled, "I will Dad, I promise."

"Uh oh, a promise like the one when you promised to stop eating all the marshmallows out of the Lucky Charms box before I got one promise?"

"No Dad, for reals this time."

Dad then sprung up and reached his right hand down to haul me up.

"Enough with the heavy stuff, race you to the gift shop Gin Gin! I'll buy you the tackiest lobster souvenir you can find!"

I had no clue at the time that Dad's days were numbered too. How could I have known that I would look back on that afternoon over and over and try to call up the sound of his voice and the touch of his hand as we scampered up the smooth rocks from the lighthouse?

That same ridiculous squeezy lobster keychain with the horrid googly eyes that Dad purchased at the gift shop all those years ago, the one that had held my house keys ever since, was being waved in my face when I finally came to on the floor of Homeroom A.

National News
@news4you

#BREAKINGNEWS: HS shooting unfolding now in Ontario. Students, staff in lockdown. Multiple weapons, possible bombs #education #breakingnews #nationalnews #schoolviolence #gunviolence #wearefollowing #staytuned

10:38 AM–April 28, 2019. Ottawa ON
♡ 897　⟲ 1056　♡ 701

Chapter 8

Blackouts were not unusual for me. In fact, I was the reason that dodgeball was forbidden in our school district. When I was in elementary school and the principal offered a reward to the entire student body for winning sports, or placing in the district spelling bee, or for volunteer or food drive efforts, we would all vote on a reward. Dodgeball always seemed to win out. There was a kind of hedonistic, *Hunger Games* obsession with dodgeball. We loved the brutality of it, the opportunity to target and get back at those who had wronged us, to trap our classmates in a corner, sniveling and begging, and then knock them clean off their feet with a whack from the giant rubber ball.

The year that I was in grade four, we had an all-day dodgeball tournament as a school-wide reward for clearing all of the rubbish in the schoolyard. During that tournament, Jace lobbed one at me, nothing too severe, but enough to knock me backwards, a stream of spit flying from my mouth as the ball hit me right in the solar plexus and knocked the wind out of me. My head slammed backwards into the glass bricks of the gymnasium wall and all went black in my world. My best friend was convinced I was dead and had a severe panic antic. An ambulance was called, for both of us, and I eventually came to, but dodgeball became a thing of the past. I became the infamous "Dodgeball Ginny" for a few years, but luckily, that moniker faded over time; it didn't stick to me like poor Boot Snack's nickname.

"C'mon Ginny, wake up!" Kayla implored, trying to keep her voice low but loud enough to rouse me.

She was waving Dad's lobster keychain in front of my face, and snapping her fingers, trying desperately to get my attention and bring me back from my memories, back to reality. I could see the lobster's googly eyes up close, magnified and slightly grotesque, and then all went black again. I could hear the urgency in Kayla's quivering voice for a moment, and then back to silence. All of a sudden, I heard a loud *THWACK* and felt a sharp sting on the side of my face.

"Hey!" I sat upright and confronted Kayla. "What'd you hit me for?!"

"Oh, thank God! Sorry Ginny, you kept fading in and out and I was worried you would never come to. I can't do this day on my own. I need you!"

"Damn, Barbie," I exhaled. "You pack a punch. Who knew?"

Kayla looked confused.

"Barbie? Is that what you think of me? A little Freudian slip there, Ginny? Not nice."

"Sorry," I looked away. She had just brought me back. Maybe I could be nicer? Maybe she wasn't just a vacant airhead screaming cheers and flashing her butt? Dad had always said I judged too quickly.

"My bad, Kayla. It won't happen again."

It was hard to kick the habit of thinking of her as a Barbie, even though my first impression was probably not accurate. Kayla was smart and beautiful and tough as nails, and I could kinda, maybe, see us hanging out if we survived this day.

Kayla held out half of a white Kit Kat bar and popped the other half in her mouth.

"Here have some."

I let my piece lie under my tongue and begin to slowly melt. My eyes rolled back in my head, in a good way for once, as I savored the smooth chocolate, my first food of the day. "Oh my God Kayla, that was so good!" I groaned.

"Ssshh," she whispered. "I don't need anyone to know I have chocolate just yet. They might go all *Lord of the Flies* on me if they get desperate. But you looked like you needed some sugar in a bad way."

"Yeah, I did. I'm known to black out if I haven't eaten, or if it's that time of the month, or if I bang my head. That piece of Kit Kat is all I've had today. So, thank you."

Kayla waved it off.

"No worries. I'm a chocoholic; always have a stash somewhere nearby. Got the ass to prove it," she gestured at her perfect butt. I sat up a little straighter trying to conceal mine underneath me. Gawd, what must she have been thinking of my cottage cheese butt? And why did I even care what she thought?

"Good to know." I smiled. "I guessed you might have a sweet tooth from the Wonka wallpaper on your phone."

"Oh, that!" she giggled. "*Charlie and the Chocolate Factory* was my favorite book growing up. My Gran was a librarian, and whenever she visited I begged her to read it to me. And I loved the Willy Wonka movie too, the original Technicolor version, not that creepy Johnny Depp mess."

I'm sure by this point my mouth was hanging open. This day just got curiouser and curiouser. I decided to confide in this Full o' Surprises Barbie.

"Funny thing, Kayla. *Chocolate Factory* was my favorite childhood book too. Despite my name and my parents' best efforts, I couldn't get enough of it. Don't get me wrong, the *Harry Potter* books are great, I get the whole wizards and spells and wands fascination, but there was just something about rivers of chocolate and fudge rooms that fascinated me. Spoke to my sugar obsession I guess."

Kayla looked at me with squinty eyes, as if she was sizing me up. Maybe I wasn't quite who she'd assumed I was either. *Rein it in, Ginny. Verbal diarrhea about your favorite topic isn't pretty. Scares people off. And you actually need this girl's help. At least for today!*

"Before she turned out my bedside lamp Gran would always recite her favorite Gene Wilder line from the movie," Kayla slowly whispered, clearly remembering something bittersweet.

"We are the music makers," Kayla started.

I cut her off and finished her thought with, "and we are the dreamers of the dreams."

Kayla just stared at me. Yep, I definitely wasn't who she'd expected either.

Shaking her head slightly as though she wasn't quite sure how to proceed or what to say, Kayla glanced down at my left arm and then looked me in the eye. I hadn't been aware until that moment that I had been repeatedly gouging an old cut scar on my forearm with my fingernails while we'd been talking. I had succeeded in opening the wound, and it was now bleeding.

"You sure you're okay?" she asked.

"Yeah," I reassured her. "It's hard to explain to people. No one else gets it."

"Try me," she whispered as she patted my left hand. "I'm a pretty good listener. And a kick-ass medical professional, as you now know," she joked.

"Um, okay," I muttered. *Here goes, putting it all on the line here, Barbie. Be kind.* "When I cut it kind of feels like I'm frozen in time, removed from the situation, and it takes me out of whatever I'm struggling with in the moment. And then when the cuts scar over I kind of like how they look. Battle scars, I guess. Or proof that I have survived? Pride, maybe? Then when the cuts start to disappear, I have to freshen them up. And they're mine too, you know? Something only I know and I can control."

My trust issues kicked into full gear as I suddenly realized I was revealing way too much to someone who was pretty much a complete stranger the day before, someone I would never normally even say hello to, a cheerleader!

"Never mind," I apologized. "I bet I sound completely nuts."

"No, no, no!" Kayla stopped me, "I kind of get what you're saying. I can see how it could make you feel that way, and how it could become a habit. But you do know you can't keep doing it, right?" she asked softly. "The cuts could get infected. And it's really just a temporary fix for something that's hurting you that you really should work on. Not that I'm an expert or anything. Just a concerned friend."

A concerned friend? I had not seen that coming. But it felt good. Maybe we would become friends if we made it out of this room. Stranger things have happened. All the gadgets on Star Trek became real things. A reality show star became President of the US ... And there was a shooter on a rampage in my high school hallway. In sleepy little Southwestern. Maybe nerdy ole Ginny Bartholomew and a cheerleading Barbie could become friends.

"Thanks," I told her. "My mom would love you. She's always on my case to stop cutting, checking my arms when she thinks I'm not looking. She thinks I'm hurting myself because my dad died unexpectedly and I never got over it."

"I'm sorry about your dad," Kayla offered. "But I think we have enough blood in this room already today without you creating any more. What if, when you want to hurt yourself, you tell yourself that it isn't your arm you're cutting but that it's your mom's or a friend's or even mine? Would that help you to ease off?"

No one had ever suggested Kayla's strategy to me before, and she did have a point about the blood in the room already.

"I might give it a try," I told her. "Thanks."

"Alright," Kayla started to lift herself up into a crouching position, "I think we should do some triage, check around the room and see how everyone's doing. At the vets' hospital I have to do that in the ER sometimes, ever since Stretchergate."

I vaguely remembered Stretchergate from a few years ago. Larry Groenewegen was a local veteran, a Dutch immigrant to our town after World War II, and everyone called him "Ladder Larry" because he had ladders propped up all over his house and was constantly climbing up on his roof to sit and look out over the houses. The guy was never content on *terra firma*. He fell off many times but it never seemed to affect him. After one particularly hard fall he took himself to the ER at the main hospital to get checked over. Ladder Larry waited all day to see a doctor and eventually just curled up on a stretcher in the hall outside the ER for a nap. They found him dead on that stretcher after he'd been waiting there for eleven hours. He'd had a brain bleed. Larry hadn't had a family doctor; they were scarce in our town. His death made our little local news and then got picked up nationally and was even covered on CNN. Mom said it was a "shameful testament to the state of healthcare and overcrowded hospitals." I thought it was just really sad.

"Let's go up and down the rows and just see if anyone needs help," Kayla suggested crouch-crawling off down the first row. Suddenly aware that I was subconsciously starting to gouge at my scars again, I balled both hands into fists and followed Kayla. *Damn Barbie, you are one calm cool piece of work. Wish I could say the same for myself.*

National News
@news4you

#BREAKINGNEWS: @SouthwesternHS still locked down. Interviews with parents at 11. Unconfirmed reports of casualties #education #breakingnews #nationalnews #schoolviolence #gunviolence #wearefollowing #staytuned #SouthwesternStrong

10:59 AM–April 28, 2019. Ottawa ON
♡ 704　⟲ 856　♡ 817

wasn't quite sure what Kayla and I would find as we moved around the room, but a part of me was preparing for a bloody, chaotic no-man's-land battlefield scene, even though my rational brain knew the shooter had never been in the room. The first row of desks we crawled along was dead quiet. Each desk had a student underneath, sitting or lying down, and most were either tracking the drama on the news on their phones or texting or playing games for distraction. I made a mental note to tell Mom about the irony of the situation if I saw her again. Mom was always arguing with me that video games desensitized people and that they had a hand to play in the violence in the world, but today those games were calming people and bringing peace during a violent event. Maybe I could finally win an argument with Mom. We moved on to the second row and checked on the huddled masses there. Kayla waved me over to one of the other cheerleaders, Keira maybe, or Kelsie, who did not look good at all.

"Kelsie, you okay?" Kayla leaned down towards the pony-tailed lump cowering under the desk. She gently grabbed Kelsie's wrist and checked her pulse. Kelsie didn't respond.

"Kelsie, talk to me," Kayla implored, getting right in her face.

"I ... I ... I can't do this, Kayla," she finally responded. "I need to get out of here. I can't take this. We are all going to die!

I know it! I'll never go to prom, I'll never walk down the aisle with my dad, and I'll never have kids or teach them to cheer!"

With each *never*, Kelsie got more frantic and agitated, her voice rising to a high-pitched squeal that would've sent dogs running. She must have been holding it all in until we came along and spoke to her.

"You are going to be okay, Kelsie. Right, Ginny? We will all get out of here and back to normal really soon," Kayla said as she turned to me. "Tell her, Ginny."

"Um, yeah," I whispered leaning down to Kelsie. Had Kayla not noticed my crap bedside manner? Did my bloody arm not scream, "disturbed girl who can't help others?!"

I don't know what came over me or why, but I pulled my phone out of my pocket and swiped through to a dog video I had saved.

"Look, Kelsie. This is my new puppy, uh, Roger. He's a Bernese mountain dog and six weeks old; he will be huge before you know it. We pick him up at the breeder tomorrow. There's no way I'm not getting out of here to pick up Roger. I've wanted a puppy forever and my mom finally relented. Look at him with his little squeezy frog. Have you ever seen anything cuter?"

Kelsie latched onto my phone with a death grip and brought it close to her face. Her eyes lit up as she watched the video.

"OMG, he's adorable. I have a teacup poodle. Her name's Coco. Well it's really Penelope Vanna Lacroix, her official registered name, but we call her Coco. She'd be devastated if I never came home."

"Well Coco will see you again, no worries. I'm sure we will get the all clear to leave here very soon," I lied. I reached over for my phone and tried twice to pry it out of her hands, but Kelsie would not let go. I gave up.

"You keep my cell safe for me, Kelsie? Just be careful, the battery is dying so I don't know how long it'll last."

Kelsie was staring at the screen; I had been forgotten and dismissed. Classic cheerleader. If Mom texted me again, I wouldn't be able to reply. But maybe she'd forgive me afterwards if I told her it was for a good cause. She was always lecturing me to pay it forward and give back. "Be the good in the world, Gin!" was her mantra.

"Look at you, Joan of Arcing all over the place. Kudos!" Kayla teased as we moved away from Kelsie. "Can I come meet your puppy when you get him?"

"Oh, Roger?" I chuckled, "That was actually just a dog video off YouTube that Owen sent me last week. We sometimes trade funny pet videos, farting potbelly pigs, goat yoga, cats trapped in tiny boxes, highbrow stuff like that. I'm severely allergic to dogs and cats."

"Whoa!" Kayla was impressed. "Well played, Ginny. You totally talked her off the ledge back there. Powerful you have become, the dark side I sense in you."

This time I tried to hide my surprise at the many sides of Kayla and took it in stride.

"Ah, I do love a good Yoda quote. Why thank you, oh wise one," I joked.

I followed Kayla over to the third row. The first desk at the front of the row was empty. That was odd since Max Jackson usually sat there and I knew I had seen him arrive to class before the bell. But there was no one under that desk.

Max was hard to miss. I hadn't grown up with him; he had arrived in our town for grade nine. And oh, what a splash he'd made. Max had a slow, sexy swagger, the kind that some are just born with, and it made all teen girls swoon. Max's jet black hair was longer than most guys, always perfectly styled off his forehead and swept back at the sides. Mom saw his picture once on my Instagram feed and said he had "Dylan McKay hair" from the original *90210* series, a 90s show I hadn't yet sampled. I

Googled Dylan McKay and saw that Mom was right. Max dressed like he had just stepped out of the pages of a men's fashion magazine, ripped jeans and tight tees, and he had the chiseled abs to boot. He usually sported a strategic five-o'clock shadow and no blemish would ever dare to appear on his ivory skin. So basically he was a perfect specimen—if you like tall, dark, and handsome. And if you're gay.

Max was out long before he arrived at our school. His first day here he sported an "I'm gay, what's your superpower?" tee while PeeWee trotted him around on a school tour like a prize pony. I'd had to hand it to him, his shirt was a super effective way to get it all out there and over with. But his pride in his homosexuality didn't stop girls from fawning over him and attempting to convert him. If anything, it made Max more of a challenge. Not a challenge for me though, as I was all about curly haired brunets. One in particular.

"Wasn't Max here earlier?" I asked Kayla.

"Yup, I saw him. I'm sure we'll find him in one of these rows," she whispered.

We moved past a few more classmates who were on their phones texting. Some wore earbuds in an attempt to remove themselves from what was unfolding outside the classroom and so were thankfully distracted, for the time being, from the distant pops that sounded off randomly elsewhere in the school. When we came to the last desk in the row, we found one of the Nerds, Rodney, curled up in the fetal position.

Kayla tapped him on the shoulder to ask, "You okay, Rod?"

He nodded his head but kept staring straight ahead, his face pale and his eyes glazed over behind his Coke-bottle glasses.

"You sure?" Kayla prodded. "You know we are all going to be fine, don't you? We'll be out and home before you know it. I saw online that the all clear should be any time now," she lied.

Rodney suddenly lashed out with one arm and pushed Kayla away.

"Leave me alone!" he blurted, a little too loudly. "I'm fine!"

Kayla turned to me and mouthed, "Shock."

I lifted my hands in the air with the universal gesture for "who the hell knows" and we moved on.

We found couples consoling each other, some groups of girls clinging together, and even one boy having a snooze under his desk. There was also a group of three on the floor beside a desk holding hands in a circle, mouths moving in silent prayer. Everyone was coping in their own way.

When our rounds brought us back to Owen's desk, we found Max huddled underneath it with him. The two guys hadn't seen us as we crawled over. Owen's eyes were still closed, and Max was holding Owen's hand and whispering something in his ear. It struck me as a little odd for a second, but I figured Max probably had a comforting bedside manner like Kayla's. I knew he was usually a calm, cool guy.

"How's Owen doing now?" I leaned under the desk to ask Max.

"He's a trooper," he said. "He's keeping a tight grip on his wound, but he seems to drift in and out when I talk to him. Don't ya, O?" he said a bit louder hoping Owen would respond. Nothing.

"I can take over if you like," I offered. "Maybe you and Kayla could go check on MJ and Miss Jones, Max. We haven't checked on them yet and MJ is probably still a mess. And check on Jace maybe. I don't think I have it in me to care how he's doing. We deliberately skipped his desk."

"That's okay," Max replied. "I'm right where I need to be." He looked at me pointedly.

"Oh ..." Kayla exhaled.

"No, it's okay," I insisted. "Owen and I are tight. I'd like to be here when he opens his eyes. He needs me."

"Um, Ginny? Maybe we should go check on MJ. C'mon I think Owen's in good hands with Max." Kayla's voice sounded weird all of a sudden, high-pitched and strained. *What's your problem, Barbie? Trying to separate Owen and me so you can have him for yourself? No frickin' way, girl.*

"No, I got this," I told them. "Stand down, Kayla. Owen will want me here. It's breaking my heart seeing him like this. And when he comes around, I might finally ask him to prom. Stuff like this forces us to stop putting things off. Live in the moment, tell your people you love them, right?"

I looked up at Kayla and Max. Kayla was looking at me like I was the one who was wounded, and Max had gone back to staring at Owen's ghostly face.

"Gin, I think Max is Owen's people," she whispered to me.

My head snapped back like I was back on the dodgeball court. That's what was going on here? I was such an idiot! My Owen was gay?! And Kayla knew before me? No, not possible. Maybe he was bi and I still had a chance?

"Th ..." My voice broke as I tried to speak. "That true, Max? You two are a couple?" I asked, already knowing the answer but having a helluva time processing it. Max looked up at me with the same pitying face as Kayla and nodded his head.

"We are," he said. "I know Owen struggled with telling you he's gay, but he just wasn't ready to tell anyone, Ginny. I've been trying to help him come out, but he'll do it in his own time. We have been very careful about our time together. I'm sorry you found out like this."

I never in my wildest dreams thought that Owen had friend zoned me all this time because he didn't like girls. Maybe because he hadn't yet realized I was the love of his life or maybe because he was hesitant to move from childhood friends to BF and GF. Or maybe he didn't know how to make the first move. But, gay?! Never.

I was stunned. No, stunned didn't even come close. I was blindsided. The kind of blindsided where you can't breathe, like you've been sucker punched. It was a physical sickening feeling, realizing that one of the constants in my life actually wasn't a constant at all. It struck me that maybe this was how children felt when their parents sat them down for the "Mommy and Daddy are getting a divorce because we don't love each other anymore but we still love you" speech. The ground shifts and you start to question who you are and whether your relationships with people are even real. How could I not have known? What signs had I missed? Man, I had to hand it to him. Owen was quite the actor. Oscar-worthy performances. Or was I just a clueless idiot? Most likely, the latter. I tried to keep my embarrassment from showing on my face and started to move past Max towards Kayla.

"No worries, Max," I lied. "I was just messing with you just now. I kinda guessed as much about Owen. The signs were all there, right? I was trying to give him space to tell me on his own. Owen and I are just good friends ... buddies. You watch your man and we'll go check on MJ."

Kayla looked me in the eyes, and when I tried to avoid her gaze, she grabbed my chin and brought me back.

"You couldn't have known, Gin. I don't think anyone knew other than Max, and now you and I." She let go of my chin and I angrily turned my head away from her pitying gaze. She reached down to grab my hand.

"I can see you had more than friend-feelings for Owen, but it wasn't meant to be. Don't beat yourself up about it. Owen probably didn't want to hurt you."

"Don't, Kayla!" I pushed her hand away. "I can't even right now. I'm fine. Just drop it and let's go check on MJ."

The truth? My heart was shattering into a million pieces. And I suddenly didn't really care whether or not we made it out alive. I left Owen and Max together and followed Kayla as she crawled over to check on MJ.

Just as I reached her, the stillness in the room was broken with a violent rattling of the classroom door handle. Someone was trying to get in.

Jace Goodwin
@TheGoodWinner

Got classroom locked down Chillin. SWPD got this Shooter gonna die Gonna kick Northwests butts this friday on da field!! #Mondays #wegotthis #staycool #notreadytodie #footballforlife

11:01 AM–April 28, 2019. Southwestern High School
♡ 98   ↻ 145   ♡ 333

Chapter 10

The silence in the room was deafening, pierced only by the sound of the door shaking as the person on the other side tried to get it open. Once, twice, three times they pushed down forcefully on the outer handle, trying to get in. With the third jarring attempt one of my classmates called out, "We're in here! HEL—"

Now I know cheerleaders are athletes, and anyone could tell that Kayla was in peak physical condition, but damn that girl can move! She sprang to life and threw herself in the air and clear across a desk, landing on Gregg with two Gs and pinning him to the ground. She clamped her hand over his mouth before he could even finish his cry for help.

"SSHHH!" she whispered loudly, addressing everyone in the room. "No one make a sound! We don't know who it is out there."

MJ began whimpering beside me and I enveloped her in a bear hug, pressing her face against my chest to snuff out the noise of her cries.

"No, MJ. We can't make a peep. I've got you."

The entire Homeroom A froze. We all crouched lower, collective breath held, waiting to see whether the door would open and who would come through. Would it be rescuers or killers? Would shots sear through the metal door? None of us had a clue but everyone seemed to be following Kayla's lead and preparing for the worst. After what seemed like half an hour, but was probably only a minute or two, we heard rattling farther off. Someone was at the next door down the hallway trying to get into Homeroom B. Then after another minute or two, a small eternity as we waited to learn our fate, we could hear the large double doors at the end of the hall open and then close, the hinges in need of some oil.

"Okay, guys," Kayla announced. "I think they're gone."

The collective exhale was intense.

I released MJ, who had become a limp rag doll in my arms, and leaned back to look her in the eyes.

"You okay?"

MJ didn't respond. She was looking at me, but at the same time, she wasn't really there. I shook her by the shoulders, trying to get a response.

"MJ! MJ! Talk to me, girl"

MJ blinked and looked me in the eye; she was back.

"S ... s ... sorry, Ginny," her voice shook. "I'm not doing so hot. I'm feeling a little bit claustrophobic in here, ya know?"

"I know," I said. "But I'm sure it won't go on much longer and then we'll be out. I haven't really been looking online to see what's happening, but Kayla is, and she said the police and SWAT are out there doing what they can. You can see the red lights flashing through the window blinds if you stretch up a little bit."

MJ poked her head up past the desktop, looked over at the windows, and then crouched back down.

"This kinda stuff, violence, shootings ... even just seeing it on the news ... it really stresses me out. I have anti-anxiety meds I can take that help, but they're out in my locker. My mom is a mess worrying about me. Keeps texting constantly. I finally just had to shut off my cell. She actually makes it worse."

"Yeah it's tough for them outside too. They're feeling helpless, I'm sure," I said.

"I lied to Mom," MJ confided", and I never do that. Told her I'd taken my meds and that I was chill."

I realized that lying to her mom was a big deal to MJ, something she felt very guilty about. I couldn't really relate; since I'd started cutting, the lies rolled off my tongue very easily. I made a mental note to maybe work on that when I got out. Now that I had MJ talking, I felt like I should keep her talking and keep her lucid. Trouble was I couldn't really think of what to talk about. I knew nothing about this girl and had no clue if we even had anything in common.

"I had a friend who took anti-anxiety meds. They really helped." I started without thinking. *Ugh! Nice one, Gin. Talk about her medications that she probably didn't want anyone to know about. Idiot.*

"They do help," she replied, not noticing my faux pas. "I've been taking them for a few years now, since my dad left."

Oh, no. I realized I had opened up a can of worms. Kayla might be an expert at comforting and consoling, but I wasn't. I was just winging it in her absence. Still, MJ did seem to be more engaged. She had stopped nervously tugging on the gold cross suspended around her neck, so that was a start.

"Oh," I said. "My dad died a few years ago. It's hard not to have him around. I'm sure you miss yours too." I was doing my best at bedside manner but probably failing miserably.

"Actually, not really," MJ explained as an embarrassed blush came over her face. "He was not a nice man, Ginny."

I didn't know how to respond to MJ's confession. So I didn't. Awkward! I looked around to see if Kayla was on her way back and could rescue me, but she wasn't. I was in uncharted territory with MJ, but then I remembered how my therapist, Dr. Lee, would often just go quiet when we were talking about sensitive stuff; she would let me talk and get it out. Maybe that's what MJ needed.

MJ continued. "He did a few tours overseas, and when he came back, he was always angry, flying off the handle, hurting my mom. He drank a lot too, which didn't help. Mom and I never knew what to expect with him."

MJ stopped talking and seemed to be retreating into herself again and reliving old painful memories. That wasn't good.

"I'm sorry you had to go through that, MJ," I patted her hand.

"Yeah," she said. "The worst was one night when he'd already given Mom a shiner and then left to go to the pub up the road. Mom decided to finally stand up to him, so when he came back, Mom made me hide in my bathroom while she confronted him. Told him the cops were on the way and to get out. That made him even madder, and he told Mom that he wasn't leaving without me. He came into my room and started pulling on my bathroom door. I had locked it from the inside and was crouched in the tub trying not to breathe too loud."

"Oh my God, MJ," I whispered.

"So today is kind of bringing that all back, you know? Feeling kind of trapped and scared. Do you think the shooter will be back for us? Or do you think he's used up all his bullets?"

I wasn't sure how to respond. I'd seen enough shootings in the States to know that most school shooters could be prepared and armed to the teeth, and Mom had mentioned bombs even in her texts.....but MJ didn't need to know that. I decided to flex my expert lying skills and try to reassure MJ. She obviously steered clear of news programs, so I could probably get a few past her.

"I don't think so, MJ. I've been counting shots and there's no way he has any left. Besides, whoever was outside our door has obviously moved on. We were so quiet they'd assume the room was empty, I'm sure."

"That's good," she breathed a sigh of relief.

"You're doing great." I put on my best reassuring smile, hoping I didn't actually look like Heath Ledger's Joker. "If you can keep it together for a bit longer, you'll soon be able to get to your locker and your meds, and we will all get to go home, safe and sound."

"Thanks Ginny," she whispered. "Sorry to unload on you like that. I know we aren't friends, I don't really have any close ones, but I kinda felt like I could talk to you just now and you'd understand."

"Of course, MJ," I said. "Anytime. I'm flattered that you trusted me with something so personal. I'm glad I was able to help make you feel better."

"You did," MJ replied. "When we get out I'll make you a Toblerone cheesecake, my specialty. Bet you didn't know I could bake? Blue Ribbon winner three years in a row at the Southwestern County Fair," she boasted as the blush crept back across her cheeks.

"I did not know that!" I said, surprised. "I have a wicked sweet tooth. Can't wait to try it! Thank you."

Just then Kayla came around the side of the desk and joined us.

"Did I hear the word Toblerone?" she asked.

"Kayla's another chocoholic, MJ," I explained. "You'd better make two cheesecakes when we get out."

"Will do!" MJ seemed pleased.

Kayla gently pushed me off to the side and back under my own desk where we flopped back down and allowed ourselves a moment of rest to regroup.

"Jeez Kayla, that was quite the Matrix move you pulled back there to silence Gregg!"

"Thanks," she said. "Those Jocks are so clueless! I get that we're all freaking out in some way, but man, couldn't Jace have silenced him? He was right beside him."

"Yeah," I agreed. "If that was the shooter, thank God he didn't hear Gregg or decided not to bother with trying to get in here!"

Kayla reached in her back pocket, pulled out another white

Kit Kat bar, and broke it in two to share without anyone else noticing. I placed it right under my tongue and relaxed as it started to melt. It really was the best thing I'd ever tasted.

"I'm imagining it's a Harvey's grilled chicken on a multi-grain bun, mayo, lettuce, tomatoes, and extra pickles, and frings on the side," she smiled at me.

"Oh, I'm currently savoring my mom's homemade mac and cheese, with extra old cheddar, and her sticky toffee pudding to follow," I said, joining in the daydream.

"Harvey's caramel pie for me all the way," she countered. We sat there quietly enjoying the respite and the chocolate and the food porn swirling in her minds until Kayla broke the silence.

"Crap!" she sat up suddenly. "We forgot to go back and check on Miss Jones! C'mon, Gin."

I swallowed the last of my Kit Kat and set off in a crawl after Kayla.

"Back to reality," I moaned. "You really are a tough task master, Barbie."

She looked back at me, feigning annoyance, and I winked at her.

"Okay, okay, said with love?" I gave her my most sheepish grin. "You're stuck with me now. We either die in here together or become besties outside together."

"Such a drama queen, Weasley," she teased. "Who knew?"

Gregg Budds
@buddsandsuds

Pray for us!! This can't be happening @SouthwesternHS
What is wrong with people?? #getmeouttahere
#notreadytodie #braveishard #footballforlife
#iloveyoumomanddadandmandy #seeyousoon

11:18 AM–April 28, 2019. Southwestern High School
♡ 96   ↻ 255   ♡ 411

Chapter 11

We hadn't crawled three feet when shots rang out.

POP!

POP!

Two shots, pinging off our door. Everyone raced back to safety under their desks, and those who hadn't ventured out cowered tighter underneath the flimsy wooden barriers. After the two blasts the room was completely silent.

POP!

Another shot. This one seeming to hit its intended target and blasting its way into the door handle. The handle shook and a chunk of metal broke off, flying through the air at breakneck speed. With that final blast Rodney crawled out from under the desk beside me and stood up.

"COME ON IN! COME AND GET US! WE'RE ALL GOING TO DIE ANYWAYS. GET IT OVER WITH!" he screamed.

I took a page from Kayla's book of heroics and scurried out from under my desk. I propelled myself into the air, and tackled Rodney, bringing him to the ground underneath me. I clamped one hand over his mouth and whispered, "Sshhh!"

I lay on top of him, spanning the length of his wiry little Nerd body and pinning him beneath me.

"Not one word, so help me. Not a peep."

Another shot rang out, this one making contact to the left

of the doorknob but not breaking through. Out of the corner of my eye I saw a blur as someone ran for the door. What the hell was wrong with these people? Am I the only one who didn't have a death wish?

I turned my head away from Rodney's face to get a better look at the door. It looked like ... Kayla? It was Kayla! She was lying on her stomach doing something to the bottom of the door.

"Kayla, come away!" I stage whispered. "Kayla!"

She turned back towards me and held a finger to her lips to silence me. With her other hand she held up a small brown wedge. Kayla then went back to what she was doing, wedging the rubber door stop under the middle of the door. It finally dawned on me. If the shooter was able to shoot the entire door handle out, or get the door to open somehow, the wedge would possibly hold it shut from our side. The door stop just might give us a little layer of extra protection. She must have figured it was worth trying.

"I'M COMIN' IN AND NO ONE IS WALKING OUT OF THERE!"

The shooter was up against the door yanking on the loose door knob with one hand and pounding on the middle of the door with the other. Kayla scurried backwards, away from the door and under a nearby desk.

"GO AHEA—" Rodney started to respond through my fingers, but I clamped down as hard as I could, cutting off his air. I pushed down so hard that I slammed Rodney's head back into the hard floor, and I gave him my most threatening glare. He shut up. His eyes bulging out. I let off a little on my grip so that he could breathe again. I'd be damned if I was going to let this Nerd get us all killed.

From the other side of the door we could all hear a ratcheting sound and the ping of small items hitting the floor. I don't know how I knew it, but I was pretty sure the shooter was reloading his gun.

"Got some special ones for you lot," he cooed through the door like a madman talking to a baby. His voice was unfamiliar to me. "They'll put you all out of your misery and you won't have to try to be quiet anymore. Now just open up and let me in so I don't have to waste anymore on the door."

Rodney started to shift underneath me, trying to wiggle free. He shook his head from side to side in an attempt to break from my clutch so that he could call out. His pupils were huge as he stared at me in complete terror.

"No," I whispered. "Stay still. Not a sound."

"Come out, come out wherever you are," the shooter teased. "Don't make me come in there!"

POP!

POP!

POP!

More shots, but quieter this time. Farther away. *Please don't let there be another shooter!*

The shooter cursed under his breath and we could hear him take two heavy steps back away from our door. Then silence. No one moved, no one took a breath.

POP!

We heard the thump of his footsteps echo down the hall as the shooter started to break into a run. Whatever was happening, whether it was another gunman firing shots or the police drawing him out, this shooter was leaving the hallway. It was just like in those messed-up, tear-jerker nature movies; bigger prey had appeared, and the beast was now backing away from the poor wounded gazelle. Worst part was, we were the wounded gazelle.

I waited for what seemed like a half an hour, but what was probably only twenty seconds, and then I eased off of Rodney while keeping my hand over his mouth. I crouched beside him.

"I am going to take my hand away now, Rod. But you cannot make a sound. Or so help me … ," I threatened. "Understand?"

Rodney nodded yes, and I removed my hand. No sooner had I done so than he bounced straight up again. He grabbed me by the shoulders and started shaking me violently.

"You bitch!" Rodney snapped. "Who do you think you are pinning me down like that?!"

He shook me so hard I could feel my brain rattling in my head, slamming against my skull over and over, the pain shooting through my forehead.

"Don't you ever touch me again, you idiot!" he screamed.

Spit was spraying off Rodney's lips and into my mouth. His eyes were bulging out of his head. His face was scarlet and covered in sweat. I could not respond. I could not get away from the death grip he had on my shoulders. I could feel myself blacking out again, the room spinning and dimming. Just when I thought my head was going to explode, the shaking stopped. I could barely make out two Nerds as they grabbed Rodney, whispering something in his ear in comforting, patient voices. They pulled him away from me and dragged him back over towards their group. I sat down cross-legged, hung my head down in my lap and closed my eyes. Someone appeared beside me.

"Ginny? Ginny? You okay?! Talk to me, Ginny!"

It was Kayla, her warm hand on my back.

"Jeez, what are you girl, some kind of fainting goat?" she muttered under her breath.

"I heard that," I said lifting my head and turning towards her. "I'm fine, thank you very much."

"Oh, sorry," she said letting out a long breath and slumping down in relief. "You are a fainter though."

The dizziness was starting to ebb, the pain in my head a dull throb, as I remembered what Kayla had just done.

"What the hell were you doing crawling around in front of the door with your little rubber door thingy and the shooter on the other side?!" I admonished her.

"I was wedging the door from the inside. I read about it in a mystery once, it stops someone on the outside from opening the door inward if the handle comes off," she defended herself.

"Well it was brilliant, and selfless, and the stupidest thing you've done today! Stop trying to be the hero. They don't always survive," I scolded her.

She ignored me and twisted around so that I could see the back of her shoulder.

"My shoulder feels sore and a bit wet, can you have a look? I might have twisted it and maybe got some of Miss Jones's blood on me by the door," she asked.

I leaned over to get a closer look. The shoulder of Kayla's shirt was ripped and there was some blood on it. A jagged piece of metal the size of a guitar pick was sticking out of her shirt, embedded in her shoulder. Kayla had been hit.

Patty Dee
@peppermintpatty

He's outside our door now! #SouthwesternStrong #notreadytodie

11:32 AM–April 28, 2019. Southwestern High School
♡ 100   ↻ 965   ♡ 597

Chapter 12

"**Um ... Kayla, you** have a piece of the doorknob in your shoulder. And it's bleeding." *Nice one. Way to break it to her gently, Ginny.*

Kayla tried to twist around as though she could see the back of her own shoulder if she twisted far enough.

"Stop twisting," I said. "Trust me, I'm not lying."

"Crap."

"You'll be okay, right? It's just a surface wound I think." I tried to reassure her. If I said it out loud maybe it would be true and not be the nasty injury I was staring at.

"Describe it to me, Ginny," she instructed. "What do you see?"

"Uh, there's some blood on your shirt and there's a triangle-y piece of metal sticking out of your shoulder."

"How big?" she asked twisting her torso again trying to see behind her.

"Stop twisting!" I scolded. "When you do that it moves. It's loose."

"What?" she asked. "You mean it's not stuck in there tight?"

"I don't know!" I said exasperated. "I'm not a doctor. It's gross, okay?!"

"Gross? What do you mean?" she asked. "Get it together, Ginny. You need to step up and help me here!"

"Ugh! It's about the size of a cookie and it has sharp edges. And it's kind of dangling a bit."

"Okay Ginny, I need you to get up real close and look and see if the skin has come apart," she said in her calm candy-striper voice.

"Do I have to?" I whined. "Can't we just leave it alone, or wrap something around it? You're supposed to leave sharp objects in, right? And then keep them tight? I think we learned that in health class or somewhere."

"If it is loose it's a different treatment, Ginny," Kayla was losing her patience with me. "Now look closely and tell me what you see."

"Damn it, Barbie," I said. I leaned in close for a better look and then jerked my head back away, my hand involuntarily going to my mouth and stifling a gag.

"What?" Kayla asked, not quite so calm anymore. "Tell me what you can see!"

I coughed a few times and cleared my throat, trying to get the image out of my head.

"Um, your shirt is all ripped away there and it's almost like a crevasse, a skin crevasse. And the metal piece is wedged into the side of it."

"Oh shit. What did you see in the open part, the crevasse?" she asked.

"It was pretty deep and there was gross white jelly at the bottom," I said.

"Damnit," Kayla exhaled.

"What's that mean?" I asked.

"It means it's a pretty big opening. I don't know how long we'll be stuck in here, and I don't want it to get bigger. It needs to be stitched up," she replied.

"I'm sure we'll get out soon, and the paramedics can stitch you up in no time," I tried to sound enthusiastic, hoping that she wouldn't say what I thought was coming next. *You better not ask me to touch that mess! I sew flowers on my jeans, not human flesh.*

"I have a needle and thread in my desk. I keep it there for Home Ec class," Kayla pointed one row over.

Of course, you do Barbie. Of course you do.

"Scoot over and get it and I'll walk you through this," she said. At a loss for words for once, and desperately trying to think of how I could get out of this without sounding like a stone-cold witch, I crawled over and retrieved the little sewing kit. When I got back Kayla was breathing a bit heavier.

"Please don't make me do this, Kayla," I implored. "I make a shitty nurse. And I don't want to screw this up and give you gangrene or flesh-eating disease or some horrible shoulder thing and then lose your arm!" I rambled on getting more hysterical by the second. "Don't make me. I'll do anything else for you but not this."

"It's fine, Ginny. You can do this easy peasy," she tried to talk me off the ledge. "Now grab that water bottle and pour some on the opening and some on the needle after you thread it. We can at least pretend like it will be sterilized," she said with a weak chuckle.

"God," I said. "This is unreal."

I threaded the needle with purple thread, just grabbing the first color in the case. I tied a knot off on the end and sat still, hoping Kayla would see the needle and realize how ridiculous this all was and change her mind.

"Okay, perfect, you knotted it. You're going to have to take the door knob bit out. Super fast! And peel my shirts back, I'll help. Then you'll squeeze the two sides of the opening together and poke the needle through my skin at one end. Just like you're sewing two pieces of fabric together. You have sewn before, right? I've seen your awesome embroidery on some of your out-fits," she flattered, pumping me up.

"I have," I answered shortly. "But not skin! I'm not Hannibal Lecter!"

"You'll do great," she reassured me. "Just be quick, for my sake. Pull the metal out and then start sewing right away."

"Oh my God, oh my God, oh my God," I breathed as I yanked the piece out of her shoulder. Kayla jerked her arm out of her button-down sleeve at warp speed and then peeled back the tee underneath revealing her bare shoulder. I poked the needle into her flesh in one swift movement. I gulped as I felt my gag reflex kick in, but nothing came up. Kayla tensed and dug her fingers into my thigh. I could tell she was holding her breath.

"Yuck!" I said with each stitch. "Yuck! Yuck! Yuck! Yuck! Yuck!"

I went as quickly as I could and tried to pretend that I was not, in fact, sewing human flesh. When I reached the end of the gash, I cut the thread with the miniature sewing kit scissors and tied a knot in the purple thread. All over within seconds. I gently eased the top of her tee back up over her shoulder. Out of sight, out of mind. Kayla gingerly slid her arm back into the sleeve of her button-down. I sat back on my haunches and let out a huge sigh.

"Done," I said and lifted my hands in the air like a chess champ who had just slammed the timer button down. "And don't ever ask me to do that again. I won't do it."

Kayla let go of my thigh, turned around, reached up and wrapped her arms around my neck. She whispered a muffled thank you into my collar bone. I reached up and tried to disentangle her.

"It's fine, no biggie. Just don't ask me again," I said, brushing it all off, willing my hands to stop shaking. *You did it. It's done. Big breath in, big breath out. Don't ever let 'em see you sweat.*

"It is a big deal," she whispered, and I could feel her tears on my bare neck. Barbie had a breaking point too. She was human after all.

"Nah," I said trying to lighten the mood. "I gave you a lovely purple embroidered daisy for good measure."

Kayla let go of me, laughed, and wiped her nose on her sleeve.

"You sure you're okay?" I asked.

"Good as new," she said. I could see the life coming back into her eyes as she straightened her back and put her virtual armor back on.

"Let's go check on Miss Jones, Ginny. She's way worse off than I am."

Casino Taxi
@casinotaxi

Free rides for those needing to get to Southwestern High Call 555–6666 #SouthwesternStrong #lookoutforeachother #taxirides

11:51 AM–April 28, 2019. Southwestern ON
♡ 542 ⟲ 991 ♡ 829

Chapter 13

We were not prepared for what we found when we got to Miss Jones. She was still lying stretched out on the floor under the windows where we had left her. Jace's jean jacket was still draped over her but it was now a deep red color, drenched in blood. Miss Jones's eyes were closed, her lips clamped shut, and a crimson pool of blood surrounded her. The blood had seeped down the length of her body to her head and the ends of her silvery blond hair were now matted in it on the floor. It looked as though someone had spilled red paint and she had fallen backwards into it. There was no one around Miss Jones, no other students by her side. Kayla quickly got to work checking Miss Jones's pulse, first at her wrist, then at her neck. This time she didn't turn back to me with a thumbs up. She leaned down and listened at her mouth, then pried it open and puffed a few breaths into Miss Jones. She stopped and listened, glanced down at Miss Jones's body.

Even I could tell by the amount of blood and the soaked jacket that Kayla should not compress, or even touch, Miss Jones's chest

"Damn it!" Kayla whispered. She then went back to breathing into Miss Jones for a few seconds, then looking at her chest, then breathing into her mouth again. I could see Kayla grimace with each movement, her shoulder must have been killing her. I realized that Kayla was trying to bring our poor Miss Jones back to life.

I crawled back a little bit and sat on my heels, giving Kayla some space to do what she needed to do. The silk scarf underneath that we had wrapped around the wound in Miss Jones's torso must have soaked clear through.

I zoned out for a bit and looked around at our classroom, reminding myself again that this was temporary and not in any way normal. We were all in lockdown and under our desks. There was a shooter in our school trying to kill innocent people, and he may very well have already killed Miss Jones and my Owen. I was now beside a Barbie who I had just stitched up, and who had become a friend I trusted completely. My Owen was gay, and we would not be going to prom together, or to college together, or getting married and starting a family.

On this one random, strange Monday, our lives were all irreversibly changing. Some would survive and some wouldn't. Those inside, and many of those outside, would struggle to deal with the aftermath of what was unfolding. Even Mrs. Turner, who Miss Jones was filling in for, would feel the effect of this day, though she wasn't here living it. How random that she was on leave and spared this tragedy? Would she be relieved? Would she feel guilty that she wasn't here with us? Would she feel safe when she returned to work, or would she even return at all? Would the school still be here after today or would bombs destroy it, or the government remove it and start fresh?

Stop it, Ginny. Enough! Get it together! I realized that I had to get out of my head, that I was spiraling out of control. My thoughts were taking me down some dark paths that were of no help to anyone. I scooted closer to Kayla who was hunched over Miss Jones. Kayla's back was heaving up and down, so I assumed she was still trying CPR. It wasn't until I leaned in closer to offer to help that I could hear Kayla's sobs.

"Whoa, whoa, what's happened Kayla?" I asked quietly.

"Sh … sh … she's gone," Kayla sobbed. "I tried to save her, but I think she was gone before we got over here."

"Oh my God," I whispered, not truly believing what was happening. "Are you sure?"

"Yes," Kayla said a little too forcefully. "I know what death looks like, Ginny!"

"Damn it," I exhaled.

"Do you have a mirror, Ginny?" she asked.

"What?" I replied. "I don't think this is anytime to worry about what you look like, Barbie!" I lashed out. I was angry at Kayla, and the shooter, and the world, even Miss Jones for getting shot.

"No, it's not for that," she said with a huff as though explaining something to a dimwitted toddler.

I handed over the bedazzled compact I kept in my back pocket that had been a gift from Mom for my twelfth birthday. Kayla opened the compact and held the mirror up to Miss Jones's mouth, which she had opened with her other hand. Kayla and I sat there motionless for a minute or two. I clued into what she was doing, having watched a few crime dramas over the years. No fog on the mirror.

"She's not breathing," I confirmed.

"She isn't," Kayla agreed, "and hasn't been for a while, I don't think. No pulse or eye movement either."

"Oh, man," I said, at a loss for any words. A few salted tears trickled down my face and into the side of my mouth as it sunk in that Miss Jones was gone. Kayla looked around and then scooted along the windows a bit to the supply cupboard. She opened one of the wooden doors and rummaged around inside. Kayla then shimmied back with a green plastic tablecloth, unfolded it and gently covered up Miss Jones. We looked at each other.

"Now what?" I asked helplessly.

"I'm not sure," she said. "This is kind of getting out of my depth now."

"Yeah. She's really dead? I mean you're sure, right?" I asked.

"Yes, Ginny. She is. I could only be more sure if I were a doctor."

"Well then, I guess you should let someone outside know. Text your mom or the news or someone?"

Kayla pulled out her phone and fired off a quick text. The tears slowly started to stream down her cheeks again.

"I told my mom," Kayla said. "She can decide who to tell. She's a nurse."

I nodded my head. This was bringing back too many awful memories about my dad. The suddenness of someone being around and breathing and full of life and then just like that, poof, gone—it was like a magician's disappearing act gone horribly wrong. I tried to recall the sound of Miss Jones's voice from this morning and pictured her rushing Owen into the classroom and running around the room barking orders and slamming down window blinds. She had done what she could to save us. She had taken a bullet for Owen and secured us safely in her classroom. A hero.

"Kayla," I whispered, "should we do something to mark her passing? I mean we can't just leave her lying under this sheet for God knows how long. And maybe we need to let the others know what happened before someone lifts the sheet."

"I don't know, Ginny. I work at the hospital and all, and I have seen people die, but I've never had anyone close to me die, no friends or family or classmates or teachers."

"Oh, lucky you," I said a little bitterly. "I have had lots of people close to me die and it sucks."

Kara Clemons
@CheerQueen

WTF Think our sub is dead under a sheet Blood everywhere When will this end? #RIP #makeitstop #notreadytodie #loveyoumommy #cheersquad

12:10 PM–April 28, 2019. Southwestern High School
♡ 325 ⇄ 1.3K ♡ 768

My Uncle Stew and my dad dying weren't my first brushes with death. When I was in elementary school, I had a best friend named Daisy. Daisy lived down the street and we had been friends since we were newborns. Our moms had met at a book club; they had both brought their baby daughters in bassinets to sleep while the women discussed the book of the month and laughed and drank wine. My mom always said that my love of reading came from those early book clubs.

"You soaked in all that literature and book talk in your sleep, Ginny," she would say. "Maybe you'll end up with a love of wine and brandy by osmosis too! You can blame me if you do."

Daisy and I went to mommy and me swim classes, Gymboree, and library story times together. When we grew into toddlers, we attended the same preschool, Southwestern Snuggles, and sometimes our moms would dress us alike and then pretend as though they were going to take home the wrong child.

"C'mon Daisy, time to get home for dinner, then bath and straight to bed," Daisy's mom would say, picking me up and hefting me over her shoulder.

"Noooo, I'm not Daisy! It's me, Ginny! You've got the wrong girl again!" I would yell, banging my fists on her back and dissolving in a fit of giggles, waiting for our moms to switch us back

Daisy and I eventually attended the same elementary school, the only one in our town. Every Labor Day weekend we would rush up to the schoolyard to check the class lists posted on the school windows to see which teachers we had been assigned to. We would clasp hands, close our eyes and count to three before looking at the list for our year, hoping we would end up together. We usually got the same teacher. There was only one year that we didn't. We were inseparable, and I think the principal knew that there would be hell to pay from both of our moms if we were split up. It wasn't worth the fuss.

Daisy and I did everything together, shaved our legs for the first time (we had no leg hair to shave, so it was a bloodbath that got us both grounded), experimented with her mom's cache of false nails and eyelashes, and taught each other how to kiss like in the movies, a skill we were eager to test out on a boy one day.

While I was an only child, Daisy had an older brother, Chad, from her mom's first marriage. Chad was often at Daisy's house and would sometimes play with us when he wasn't doing homework or cutting lawns for spending money. He'd voice the Han Solo character, really a Ken doll, when our Barbies went into outer space, and he'd hold one end of the skipping rope and tie the other end to Daisy's fence so she and I could skip together.

Chad also made us micro-nachos if he was around when I went to Daisy's house after school. Chad's famous micro-nachos consisted of nacho chips with ketchup and cheese slices on top, nuked for thirty seconds. We thought he was an ingenious chef. I knew some of the other girls at school had older brothers who teased them, bullied them, or just refused to even acknowledge they existed. Not Chad. He loved Daisy and I, and we idolized him.

Early in September the year that Daisy and I were in Miss Murphy's fourth grade class, Daisy's mom came to the school and pulled her out of the classroom. Daisy didn't want to leave as it was twenty-five-cent hot dog day at lunch, an event we all eagerly awaited, but Miss Murphy took Daisy by the hand, whispered something in her ear and they both left the room. When I got home that night, eager to tell my mom about the four hot dogs I had managed to scarf down, a new personal record, Mom cut me off quite quickly and the tears started. She told me as gently and clearly as she could that Daisy and her parents were having a tough time because Chad had fallen off his skateboard and hit his head. I asked Mom if he was in the hospital and if we could go see them all and take some Sour Cherry Blasters, Chad's favorite candies, with us for a get-well gift. Mom then got to the crux of her story; Chad had been left brain dead as a result of his fall and had not survived the day.

I was ten years old when Chad died. People didn't die in my life. I had never experienced a pet dying or a grandparent. I was stunned and a bit confused by Mom's news. How could Chad, who had been the banker when the three of us had played Monopoly just the day before, now be gone forever? How could that happen? Didn't he get to grow up and have girlfriends, kids, and a career and grow old like everyone else? I broke down in a fit of sobs, big heaving gasps, snot pouring from my nose, and I couldn't stop. When my dad came home from work, Mom left to console Daisy's mom. Dad gathered me in a big bear hug and sat beside me on the couch until I fell asleep, then he carried me upstairs and tucked me in. I still remember what he said.

"Ginny, it doesn't make any sense and it's not fair, you're totally right. Chad was a great kid. But we have to dust ourselves off and keep living. For Chad's sake. Because he doesn't get to."

I thought of that advice when Dad died, and I have tried to follow it. I've tried to live for the people who don't get to. But it sure is hard when your heart isn't in it and you're not sure you can even get up and face another day without those people.

Daisy didn't come back to school that week, or ever again. I asked Mom every day if we could go and visit her at her house, but when Mom would call Daisy's mom to ask, the answer was always "maybe tomorrow." I never got to see Daisy again. She and her mom and dad moved away that Christmas, maybe to Edmonton or Calgary. I'm not sure anymore.

I did hear rumors at school the following year that Daisy's mom tried to commit suicide with pills the Christmas Eve after Chad died and that the family had left to try and start fresh, without reminders of Chad and the tragedy. I Googled Daisy a few times over the years but found nothing. They'd vanished. Maybe it was for the best, since I wasn't sure what I would say or how we could reconnect and go back to normal anyway. I did always think of Chad whenever I had nachos or even just saw them on a menu though.

Experiencing a death when you're so young changes you forever. You never quite get over it; you never get that innocence back, that feeling of invincibility, that belief that a long life is a foregone conclusion and yours to do with as you please. Although my "lucky you" comment to Kayla was admittedly more sarcastic than heartfelt, she really was lucky to have avoided all that pain for so long. Unfortunately for Kayla, and others in Homeroom A, that grace period of innocence was up.

News Talk Radio 956
@NEWSTALK956

#BREAKINGNEWS: 9 @SouthwesternHS pupils escape from cafeteria, tell of multiple victims and heroic acts by staff & students to console and protect. Stay tuned. #education #SouthwesternStrong

12:29 PM–April 28, 2019. News Talk Radio 956
♡ 425 ⟳ 1.6K ♡ 889

Chapter 15

We knew we had to do something about Miss Jones, but we just weren't sure what.

"I know someone who might be able to help," I told Kayla. "Back in a sec."

I crawled off to MJ's desk. MJ had been worrying over a cross on a chain all morning and seemed to be much more lucid when we'd talked earlier. I wasn't religious, and my family didn't go to church, so I thought maybe MJ could do some kind of ceremony for Miss Jones. I had been out of it at my dad's funeral and didn't remember what happened that day. MJ was worth a try at least. We didn't have many options.

I filled MJ in on Miss Jones's passing, and when I saw the tears start to trickle down her face, I quickly informed her that I needed her and now was not the time to fall apart. MJ took a big breath in and seemed to center herself before crawling back with me towards Kayla and Miss Jones's body. Along the way I whispered to a few of the students, ones who seemed calm and able to handle the news, that Miss Jones had succumbed to her gunshot wound and that we were going to pay tribute to her in a few minutes if they wanted to meet over by the windows. I told each person I spoke with to pass along the message to anyone who they felt could handle it.

When we got back to Kayla she was sitting beside Miss Jones, her hand resting protectively on top of the green tablecloth.

"MJ is going to help us say a few words about Miss Jones, Kayla," I told her. "And I let a few of the others know in case they wanted to join us."

Kayla looked skeptically at me, then over at MJ. I knew she was probably wondering why the heck I would ask MJ to help out when she had been a complete mess all morning.

"You've got this, right MJ?" I said pointedly.

"I think so," she replied. "I run the Sunday School program at our church twice a month. I can think of something to say for Miss Jones."

"Great, thanks," Kayla patted MJ on the shoulder.

I had to give props to Kayla, she was awfully chill, and nothing phased her. She just rolled with the punches and got on with it. I was impressed.

MJ, Kayla, and I sat alongside Miss Jones and watched as classmates crawled over and formed a large semi-circle around us. Some of the guys lifted a few desks and carried them a bit farther away to make room for the gathering crowd, all without a sound. When it seemed like everyone who was coming had arrived, I crossed my legs and raised one hand in the air.

"I hate to have to say this, but Miss Jones was hit by a bullet as she was getting us all locked in here this morning. Her wound was pretty awful, and she didn't make it. Kayla, MJ, and I thought we should do something for Miss Jones while we are all stuck here, to thank her for being such a nice teacher this year and for s ... sacrificing herself to keep us safe today."

I stumbled on the word *sacrifice* when I pictured Owen running in the classroom door this morning and Miss Jones trying to get him inside safely. I choked up and tears started to pour uncontrollably down my face. I had been worried about MJ keeping it together and now I was the one losing it. *Get a grip, Ginny. You can fall apart when you get out.*

Kayla leapt to my rescue.

"I think what Ginny is trying to say is that we should all be grateful to Miss Jones and thank her in our own way for all that she has done for us, not just today but all year. I'll start. Whenever one of our cheer group does something amazing, we all grab hands in the center and then lift them to the sky and call their name as we let go, and I'm sure Miss Jones is looking down and watching us now."

Kayla held her hand out and everyone grabbed on.

Kayla whispered, "We love you, Miss Jones. We will see you again someday." Then we all raised our hands and let go in midair. After that, others started to speak up and recount memories of Miss Jones. One of the Jocks recalled how she had given him a free pass when he hadn't finished a paper for class because he'd been playing in a semi-final the day before. Two girls told how Miss Jones had French braided their hair at lunch one day as they chatted outside on the grass. A super timid girl who never made a peep spoke up and told how Miss Jones had lent her money for the bus and bought her lunch when her purse was snatched on the way to school. Everyone had a story, memory, or a nice comment about Miss Jones to contribute. Finally, it was MJ's turn.

"Um ... so," she started a bit nervously. "I don't really have a Miss Jones story, but I thought she was a great teacher and we were lucky to have her while we did. I am really sorry that she won't be walking out of this room with us."

MJ looked over at Kayla, unsure how to proceed. Kayla gave her a thumbs up and then waved her hand at MJ to keep talking.

"Um ... I know that now Miss Jones is in a better place, whatever you believe, a safe place," MJ's voice got stronger as she went on. "She is with the people in her life who she loved and who have passed on. She is somewhere where the sun always shines and the birds always sing. And she isn't hurting anymore."

Kayla and I exchanged a look. Was this the same girl who

had been sniveling loudly under her desk just a few hours ago, unable to move or speak?

"Wow," I whispered to Kayla. "That was perfect. I was worried she might be all churchy and preachy, but she nailed it."

"You really need to work on the judging, Ginny," Kayla half-teased. "Get to know people before you decide who they are. We aren't all what you see on the outside."

Whoa! "Thanks, Cheer Queen," I lashed out." I'll add it to my to-do list, right below getting out of this classroom alive."

Most of the group had gone back to their positions under their desks, and I decided to do the same. I'd given MJ the opportunity and confidence to lead an impromptu memorial service, and now I was getting trashed by Kayla for being judgey?! Classic. Kayla and MJ could bond over my flaws. Screw 'em.

I pulled my hoodie up over my head, lay down on my back under the ode to Jarrod and closed my eyes. *Oh Jarrod, you have no idea how lucky you were that you lived at a time when being called a wiener was probably your biggest worry at school!* I slowly dragged my fingernail along the scars on my forearm. I didn't need anyone. Owen had Max now, and Kayla could have MJ. Hell, Kayla and I hadn't even said two words to each other before this all happened. I didn't need her; I'd be fine on my own. I'd just have to wait it out under my desk until the cops let us all out.

My mind wandered and I wondered what Mom was doing and thinking at that moment. In a crisis, you wanted Susan Bartholomew on your side. She never lost it, was always cool and rational, and she always made those around her feel better no matter how it affected her. The only exception was when it came to her daughter. Since Dad died, she was super protective of me. If I so much as mentioned in passing that someone had ticked me off, Mom was on the warpath. If I coughed, she ran to the store for echinacea, lozenges, and ginger ale. When I twisted my ankle at a school dance, she refused to let me leave the couch for the entire weekend. I spent the time with my leg propped up, scented candles on the coffee table, and a steady stream of my favorite baked goods delivered from the kitchen at regular intervals. I made that treatment last as long as I could. I'm sure Mom clued in that I had recovered, but she kept on pampering me anyways.

I couldn't imagine what she was thinking while holding vigil outside, but I was sure she was keeping busy lifting others' spirits and distracting them when she could, mom-ing all over everyone but herself. I reached up and yanked a pen and scrap of paper off of the desk above my head and started writing:

To-do list ~~if~~ when we are rescued

1. *Apologize to Mom*
2. *Find Mom's bracelet*
3. *Get a new tattoo*
4. *Help Owen come out*
5. *Try to find Daisy*
6. *Get my learner's permit*
7. *Get rid of all my "stuff"*
8. *Learn a new language (Spanish? Mandarin?)*
9. *Plan a trip*
10. *Get a job (**need for #3, #8 & #9!)*

I was folding my list carefully into thirds to shove it into my back pocket when the stillness in the room was broken.

Thump.

Thump.

Thump.

Someone very strong was banging so hard on the classroom door that the windows on the other side of the room rattled. And then the screams started.

Paul Rock
@TheRock

Pray for us We will survive and fix this You okay @Kaylacheers?? @SouthwesternHS #SouthwesternStrong #hateneverwins #loveoneanother

12:52 PM–April 28, 2019. Southwestern High School
♡ 328   ↻ 701   ♡ 499

Chapter 16

bolted to a sitting position and looked around the room trying to see who had screamed. Whoever it was had quickly been silenced and all was quiet again. No one moved. The Nerds had Rodney secured in their own private lockdown huddle, the Jocks must have had Gregg secured too. The terror in the air was thick.

A voice in the hall yelled, "I'm back! You can't hide. I see all!"

Some people broke out in whimpers as we heard the shooter speak. His voice sounded scratchier this time, raw and manic. A loose cannon. He was a few feet away from us, and we were once again separated only by the door and walls. Our safe haven could easily be shattered with a single shot through the glass. Our new normal of the past few hours, patiently waiting under our desks, texting, tweeting, reassuring our friends, was wiped out, and the grim reality of our situation was thrust back in our faces.

There was the wrenching sound of metal being dragged across glass as the shooter scraped his weapon along the window in the door. He then tapped it slowly on the pane.

Tap.

Tap.

Tap.

Tap.

Then we heard him speak again, this time much calmer and slightly quieter, and for some reason I found that control even more terrifying.

"Sit tight, I'll be back for you," he said.

We all held our breath as we heard the shooter's heavy footsteps retreat. He walked slowly and deliberately, each step like thunder. When the doors at the end of the hall once again creaked shut, there was an audible exhale in the room. Another near miss. Crisis averted, for now. Who knew if and when he would be back, and if he would make good on his threat? Why had he left and spared us? Would his twisted hallway patrol bring him back to our door again?

Kayla appeared under my desk, her face pale, as I'm sure mine was, after another close brush with the shooter.

"My God, Ginny. Just when I was starting to think it might soon be over," she said.

Kayla seemed a bit defeated and definitely more scared than I'd seen her all morning.

"Yeah," I answered her. "That was like a sequel to the horror movie of his earlier appearance. Except it's real. Too real."

"I saw some tweets that say the police are trying to flush him out in parts of the school with smoke bombs. Maybe that's what sent him back down our hallway. I know some students escaped from the cafeteria too," Kayla said.

"Good," I replied. "He can't win. Do they know who it is? Cops still think it's staff?"

"Think so," she replied. "Some temp maintenance worker whose wife was going to leave him and take his kids was the last I saw online."

"Jeez, you just never know, I guess," I tried to wrap my head around the situation and, failing, turned on Kayla. "How are you feeling? How's MJ? You two besties now?"

"Oh, Ginny," she started. "I'm fine and so is MJ. I didn't mean to criticize you. I flew off at you and I'm sorry. My nerves are raw."

"I get it. I shouldn't have lashed back at you either. We aren't ourselves today, obviously."

"And MJ's actually pretty cool when you get to know her. We have more in common than I thought," Kayla revealed.

"Mm-hmm," I mumbled, still a teeny bit jealous of how Kayla had defended MJ earlier, and pegged me as judgey, accurately too. *Get over yourself already, Ginny.*

"Back at it?" she asked looked down at the thin blood trail where my fingernail had reopened an old scar.

"Now who's judging?" I asked defensively.

"Not judging, just concerned. Maybe this isn't the best day for drastic changes?" she smiled.

"Ya think?" I laughed.

"I saw some tweets from my friend who's up on the second floor. He thinks that most classes were locked down quick enough, so maybe it won't be too bad when it's all over. He's safe at least."

"Friend?" I asked with a smirk. "Something you're not telling me, Kayla? God knows I could use a distraction right about now."

"Yes, a friend," she insisted. "We've been out a few times for coffee, nothing serious. His name is Paul, he's on the basketball team ... and he's pretty hot." She blushed.

"Do tell!" I said. It was nice to feel normal for a few seconds — girl talk and gossip amidst the blood and chaos.

"Nothing to tell really. It's early days, taking it slow. He is an incredible kisser though. We were actually supposed to go to the movies tonight. I think he's going to ask me to prom."

Kayla was starting to gush just a bit, speaking quickly and unable to keep the smile off her face.

"Okay, stop," I cut her off. "Never mind, I was wrong. It's too soon. I'm still trying to figure how I went so wrong with Owen."

I'm jealous. Not ready to hear about your hot new expert kisser. Sorry."

"No worries, I get it," she said. "Hey, you could come with us if he asks me."

"I'm sure Paul would love that, third-wheel Ginny along for the ride. No, thanks. But nice of you to ask, Kayla. You really are too nice for your own good."

We sat in silence for a few minutes. At least Kayla didn't reply with a "No *you* are too nice, Ginny." That was another thing I was starting to really admire about Kayla. She told it like it was, nothing sugar coated or fake. You could really trust people like that.

"Listen Ginny, I've been thinking, maybe we need to try to move everyone away from the hallway side of the room. Just for that extra security, in case he comes back. What do you think?"

"Probably not a bad idea," I agreed. "We could get some of the guys to rearrange the desks and then try to corral everyone."

We moved around the room helping to move desks and ushering students closer to the other side and away from the inner wall. Kayla mostly pointed and directed others; she couldn't risk dislodging my fine stitchery. It was quite impressive how quiet everyone was staying; there was only an errant scrape or two from a desk leg when everyone would freeze for a few seconds and hope that the shooter wouldn't notice and return. It was much harder to usher our classmates into new positions. Some clung to their desk legs like castaways to a life raft, afraid to leave the one thing that they believed had kept them safe up to that point. We couldn't move Owen. He was still breathing but remained semi-conscious, eyes closed, not speaking. Max insisted that he would stay with Owen and kept a firm grip on Owen's hand when we suggested Owen would be fine on his own and that Max could check on him periodically. While I was still stung by Max's revelation about their relationship, I had to give it to him; if I couldn't have Owen, he seemed to be in good hands with Max. And damn, they would make a stunning couple when they were back on their feet.

Kara Clemons
@CheerQueen

He is in the hallway again! Where is SWAT??
Someone has to stop him! #terrified #notreadytodie
#SouthwesternStrong #cheersquad

12:59 PM – April 28, 2019. Southwestern High School
♡ 600 ↻ 897 ♡ 651

Chapter 17

The dynamic in Homeroom A changed. There was a noticeable buzz in the room. It could have been due to the fact that everyone was huddled much closer together under the windows, or that they felt safer as a group. Or maybe it was the fact that time was passing and the belief in a quick rescue was long gone. Maybe people were just fed up and wanted to feel less like victims and more in control. Or it was anger setting in. Students were whispering among themselves and sharing information gleaned from texts and tweets:

"I read that the shooter is dead and the cops are just waiting to remove the body and then get us out."

"I read that the Prime Minister is flying to Southwestern tonight."

"My dad said that if it goes on much longer they will call in the military."

"My uncle is a cop, he said his team won't eat or sleep until they get us out of here."

"I heard that PeeWee was the first one killed."

"CNN is live tweeting from outside, how cool is that?"

"If you want the latest use #SouthwesternStrong."

"Beyoncé just retweeted the news about us!"

Some were discussing what they'd do first when they were released — how they had a newfound gratitude for everyday comforts and routine and people in their lives. It was a nice distraction from our brutal reality.

"I can't wait to hug my cat Phoenix, and my parents and my baby brother."

"I just want my mom's lasagna with garlic bread, and a nice cold one."

"I will be stopping at 7-Eleven on my way home. Big Gulp and hot dogs, I can almost taste it."

"My stomach stopped growling hours ago; I'm not even hungry anymore. But I'd love to take a shit in my own bathroom. This one's disgusting, there's even puke on the walls."

"First thing I'm going to do is jump in my boyfriend's arms and tell him how much I love him."

And of course, there were those seeking revenge, bragging about what they would do if they had the shooter alone for a few minutes. Jace's voice was often the loudest in the crowd,

"He'll regret the day he came to my school ... he won't know what hit him ... that guy will pay ..."

All talk and bravado, empty threats from the safety of the locked classroom.

Jace's parents were both high priced attorneys in Southwestern, quasi-small-town celebrities with their shiny red convertibles sporting license plates advertising *SUE4YOU*. Their house was the largest in town, complete with an infinity pool, a go-kart track, and a guest house that was often party central for the Southwestern Sabres football team. Jace's parents doted on him and his pageant winning older sister, Joy. He had been coddled since birth, and groomed to be the perfect Ken doll, fit, athletic, smooth, and popular. Too bad he was dumb as a stick and felt the world was his for the taking, screw the consequences.

I could understand why Kayla had kept quiet about what happened with Jace. His parents would have raked her through the coals. Victim blaming was real and Jace was Teflon. When he had given another boy a black eye in elementary school for daring to call him a loser the boy and his family had been ostracized in town. The Goodwin's network had boycotted the boy's family's hardware store and they'd ultimately gone out of business. While I could totally get how Barbie Kayla would be attracted to Jace, now that I knew the real Kayla, I couldn't understand why she would ever go out with him. Hormones were a powerful thing, I guessed.

I prided myself on having a pretty good feel for people and I knew at a very young age that Jace was not someone I wanted to be around. My parents bragged about how, at the age of six, I had caught Jace trying to peek under my skirt during recess and had trapped him inside the dome shaped monkey bars until he apologized and promised to leave me alone. Except for that one spin the bottle incident, Jace and I had kept clear of each other ever since.

Faintly, among the whispered chatter, I could make out voices singing softly. I looked around the group trying to find the source. A group of students gathered in a row alongside Miss Jones tablecloth draped body. They were holding hands and their heads were bowed.

I once was lost but now am found
Was blind but now I see

I recognized the lyrics to "Amazing Grace," a personal favorite, and made my way over to the gathering. I stayed off to the side slightly and didn't reach for anyone's hand as I chimed in quietly for the last few lines.

Amazing grace, how sweet the sound
That saved a wretch like me
I once was lost but now am found
Was blind but now I see
Was blind, but now I see.

As our song ended, I looked up and noticed MJ was one of the students paying tribute, and she was looking at me.

"Ginny, you have such a beautiful voice," she said. "Soft but strong at the same time. Do you sing somewhere?"

"No," I replied, secretly pleased. "Unless you count carpool karaoke or belting out the hits in the shower."

"Your voice is incredible; you should totally join our choir. We meet every Tuesday after last period," MJ offered.

"Thanks, but I'm just a wannabe, no training. I wouldn't want to ruin your choir."

"No, really. That voice! We need you. Think about it?" MJ pleaded.

"Alright, I will," I told her. But what I would really be thinking about was who this confident girl leading her classmates in song was and what she had done with the invisible MJ who I poked with my Blundstone just this morning. Had she been in there all along? I reached around to my back pocket and pulled out my to-do list and pen and added one more line:

11. Stop Judging

News Talk Radio 956
@NEWSTALK956

#UPDATE: @SWPD say they are closing in on school shooter Live conference outside @SouthwesternHS in 10 mins #education #SouthwesternStrong #staytuned

1:05 PM–April 28, 2019. News Talk Radio 956
♡ 877   ⊔ 1.7K   ♡ 956

Chapter 18

Kayla was seated under the window ledge, cross-legged and surrounded by cheerleaders. They were whispering among themselves, ponytails bobbing like birds pecking at seeds on the ground, and I swear they smelled like cotton candy and lollipops. Her squad — Or was it a troupe of cheerleaders? Or a gaggle? Or a flamboyance? No, that was definitely a group of flamingos ... Bad Ginny — was there, even Kelsie, who seemed calmer than before but still clutched my phone. I scooted over to the group and tapped Kayla on the shoulder.

"What are you guys talking about?" I asked feeling a little excluded and wanting my new friend back.

"Oh, nothing," she said. "Trying to keep our minds off of things by reviewing a few cheers and routines. I know it sounds creepy, but we need something normal to think about. Something to look forward to, I guess"

"I get it," I said.

"Kelsie seems much better now, right?" Kayla asked. "That was really nice of you to give her your phone."

"It's weird," I said. "Usually when I don't have my phone I'm lost; I feel naked. But I haven't missed it at all today. She needs it more than I do. I'll explain to my mom later, if there is a later."

"I hope this all ends soon," Kayla said. "I don't know how long Miss Jones should be lying there. It's not exactly freezer temps in here, if you know what I mean. My shoulder is throbbing, and I'm starting to get a bit claustrophobic. Need to get out of here, get some fresh air. All the body spray mixed with sweat, and that bathroom, jeez. It's all starting to make me lightheaded!"

"Yeah, me too." I agreed. "I'm getting antsy. And salty. I'm finding myself thinking what I would do to the shooter if I had a few minutes alone with him. Tell me a story, Kayla. Distract me."

"A story? What kind of story?"

"I don't care, whatever you want. No shooters or guns or violence though. Just get me out of my head. Please?"

"Alright," Kayla sighed loudly, looking up at the ceiling trying to think of a story to tell. Okay, got one."

"Great, let me get comfy."

I scooted flat out on my back, hands under my head.

"Mentally eating popcorn with M&Ms mixed in, Coke in hand. You may begin!" I smirked.

"Okay," Kayla replied. "It's super weird telling stories in here with all that's going on, but what isn't weird about today? Here goes. There once was a very happy little girl who lived in a small town with her parents. She was adorable! Blonde haired, blue eyed, freckled. Everyone loved her and fussed over her like a little princess. She—"

"Hold up, what's her name? She needs a name." I interrupted.

"Ugh, I am not doing this if you are going to keep stopping me, Ginny. Her name was ... Beth ... alright?"

"Beth? Great. Continue."

"So Beth had the best life, a life most kids only dream of. She just had to point at a toy and her parents would buy it for her. They all took trips together to beaches and fun fairs and parks. And every Sunday the family had pancakes for breakfast and her dad would shape the batter into bunnies and Mickey Mouse heads with huge ears and chocolate chips for eyes. When Beth grew out of her crib and then her toddler bed, her mom decorated her big girl room with a princess canopy bed and a three-story dollhouse that was a replica of Beth's real house. Life was a fairytale.

"When Beth turned five years old, she started kindergarten at the local school. She was really excited to start school and knew all her letters and numbers before the first day. She could even print *Beth*, *Mom*, *Dad* and *Caesar*, the family schnauzer's name. Beth's parents always told her she was a very smart girl and that she was the nicest girl they knew. Her first few weeks at school were great. Beth loved it and she loved her teacher, Miss K.

"Then, after about a month, a couple of the kids started to notice when Beth spoke, and they would whisper to each other. Then they started to tease her. 'Beff, why you t ... t ... t ... talk like ffat?' You see, Beth stuttered. And Beth didn't pronounce some sounds right. *Th*'s came out sounding like *f*'s. *W*'s sounded like *r*'s. No one had made fun of Beth before. Her parents thought her speech was cute and that it would probably go away on its own. Beth brushed it off. She still loved school and had lots of kids to play with. She liked learning new words and learning how to read books and write sentences. Beth ignored anyone who teased her; she was too busy playing and learning.

"When Beth entered grade one the next year, things started to change. More of the kids noticed her stuttering and started to talk about it.

'You can't play with us, you talk weird.'

'Why, does Beth have to read out loud, it takes too long?'

'B ... b ... b ... b ... beff is th ... th ... thupid'

"So even though Beth loved school and learning, and she couldn't have been happier at home with her loving parents and her neighborhood friends, the teasing gradually started to get to her. Beth started to pretend to not know words in class, even though she did, so that the teacher wouldn't call on her. The happy, chatty, little girl started to speak less and worry about what she wanted to say. The teacher assumed that Beth would rather not speak in class and so she would pull Beth aside to do her reading practice at the teacher's desk, when the rest of the class was working at their desks. This actually caused more harm than good because the other students thought that Beth was getting special attention from the teacher, and the teasing got worse. Beth would hear the other's chanting 'Beff, Beff teather's pet,' but she tried not to cry or show that it upset her. She just became quieter and more timid. Happy, outgoing, energetic Beth was disappearing.

"When Beth turned six years old, her parents realized that Beth's speech was not something that she was going to grow out of quickly, and they were anxious about the changes in Beth since she had started school. Their Beth was still very smart and was reading and writing well above her grade, but she rarely read out loud or spoke or sang anymore. She became very quiet and people thought she was shy. So, when Beth started grade two, her parents asked that she start seeing a therapist who would take her out of class for half an hour each morning and afternoon. They would work on sounds, and how to fix her breathing to help with the stutter, and how to slow down. And Beth had exercises to do at home at night too.

"The other kids teased her even more about being different and getting to leave class, and they would still chase her at recess yelling 'Wun, Beff, wun.' Beth got quieter and quieter. Over the years Beth learned how to manage and hide the stutter and she learned how to pronounce her *Th*'s and her *r*'s. But the bullying and teasing stuck, and so if you had never met Beth before, you would think she was a very smart, shy girl, who didn't talk much. But you wouldn't know she'd ever had speech problems."

"Damn bullies," I interrupted.

"Sshhh." Kayla put her finger to her lips.

"During the summer between grade seven and eight, Beth

started taking gymnastics and dance classes. She loved those classes and she was pretty good at them both too. No one in the classes teased her because they didn't know her; the classes were in another town about a half hour away. Then in between grade eight and nine, Beth's dad got a new job and they moved to a town where no one knew her.

"When Beth started high school that September; she was starting fresh with new classmates who didn't know about the teasing and the stuttering. Beth joined clubs, got a job, and slowly started to come back out of her shell, like a beautiful turtle, her mom said. She made new friends and gained confidence and started to become the girl she used to be, who couldn't wait to jump out of bed and get to school each day ... and she lived happily ever after. The end"

"Until a shooter showed up at her school, right Beth?" I asked.

"Yup. You knew it was my story?" she asked, surprised.

"Pretty much from, 'There once was a happy little girl,'" I teased. "So, not the blissful early years I had assumed?"

"Nope," she said. "Gymnastics and dance really saved me and then that got me into cheering, which helped my confidence even more."

"Hmm, guess you didn't get into it for the cute skirts and the guys then? Only reasons I'd ever get on someone's back and yell 'Rah!'"

"No, and it's great exercise," she said. "I got Skylar to join too and it has been great for her confidence. She's the girl who I volunteer with as a Big Sister. You should really ..."

"Wait, wait, wait, hold up there, Cheer Squad Barbie," I held up my hand in her face. "If I hear about one more saintly thing you do, or one more hardship you overcame, I will lose my Kit Kat right here at your feet. And I might have to rethink my whole life."

I was only half-joking. I grabbed the pen and crumpled up paper out of my back pocket and added:

12. Do something good for someone else

I might not get to every item, and the list might have to change in parts, but it was a start. I held the paper up so Kayla could read it.

She looked it over quickly and then replied, "Proud of you, my friend."

I don't take compliments well, and while I was desperately trying to dial up a sarcastic retort, Kayla started quickly scrolling through her phone. She then began typing frantically, thumbs flying.

"Wow. Wow," Kayla spoke barely above a whisper.

"What's wrong?" I asked, looking around and noticing that the noise level was rising rapidly in the room and that many others were also intent on their phones, scrolling and typing feverishly.

"One sec." Kayla kept typing.

I waited patiently, picking up a few excited voices in the room and the sounds of people moving about more, coming back to life.

One one thousandth, two one thousandths, three one thousandths. It wasn't one sec. I counted out twelve secs. The longest twelve seconds of my life.

Paul Rock
@TheRock

Outside and safe! Thank you!!! Praying for those still inside and those we've lost #SouthwesternStrong #lovewillwin

1:11 PM–April 28, 2019. Southwestern High School
♡ 327 ↻ 1.6K ♡ 959

Chapter 19

Kayla looked me in the eye and placed her hand on top of
mine.

"People outside are tweeting that the shooter is dead,"
she said.

"Yes!" I said as I punched the air. "That's awesome. What did
they say?"

"Um … 'shooter may be down, self-inflicted,' 'SWPD take
out Southwestern killer,' 'SWPD preparing to get students out.'
And then my mom said that some students are already outside,
and I haven't heard from Paul in a while. Maybe he's already out?"

"I wonder how they will get us all out," I said. "It's not like
the SWPD have dealt with this before. And how will they know
if he really is dead?" I worried.

"I'm sure they know what they're doing," Kayla reassured
me. "Don't lose it now, Ginny. Not after all this."

In that moment, we heard the high-pitched wail of sirens
outside and could see flashing red and blue lights reflected in
the windows. We could hear vehicles screeching to a stop in the
parking lot and the faint hum of a helicopter.

"Things are definitely happening," Kayla said.

The others in the room seemed to be noticing too. People
were inching up and over the window sill to look out at the ac-
tivity. The noise level continued to rise and we noticed that some
had turned the volume back up on their phones and ringtones

were going off and pings could be heard as messages were exchanged.

"Shit," I said to Kayla. "You are going to have to do something. We don't even know if he's dead. Could be a false alarm or fake tweets or maybe there's even more than one shooter! We can't get stupid now!" I could feel myself starting to panic, my heart racing and my breath catching.

"Me? I'm going to have to do something? Why me?" she asked.

"Because they listen to you and you have dealt with this all day like a boss. Home stretch now, Kayla."

"Ugh," Kayla groaned, then turned to the class. "I don't think we should do anything yet, no one has sounded the all clear or contacted anyone in here about getting out."

Frustrated at the possibility of being so close to freedom but not knowing for sure, I decided to go check on Owen. Since Max's revelation, I had purposely tried to stay away, for my own sanity and to give Max some space to be with his boyfriend. I crawled over to them, Kayla shadowing right behind me, and found Max propped against the cupboards with Owen's head in his lap. Max's eyes were closed but his lips were moving. He didn't look good.

"Hey Max," Kayla said. "How's our boy doing now?"

Max roused and opened his eyes to look at us.

"Not good," he said. "He did wake up for a few minutes and take some water but then he went back to that deep sleep." Max shifted a little trying to sit a bit higher and raise Owen's head a little father up his lap.

"His nose stopped bleeding a while ago, but I think his leg wound is bleeding again," Max said.

Kayla and I looked down at Max's legs where Owen had been resting a minute ago. Max's jeans were wet with blood from the knee down. I could smell the metallic scent and could only guess at how uncomfortable it must have been for Max to be sitting in jeans sopping with blood, especially since it was his boyfriend's blood.

"Oh," Kayla said, worry in her voice. "Here Max, we need to try to stop that if we can," she said whipping off the bloody button-down she'd had on over top of her Southwestern Cheer tee. The shirt was a write-off, spattered with dark splotches of both Miss Jones's and Kayla's blood and the hole in the shoulder. "Help me lift Owen's hips a bit Ginny, so I can try to tie this around his leg," she said as she turned the shirt inside out and held the sleeves out to use for ties.

Max supported Owen with both hands under his back and I gently lifted Owen's leg while Kayla swiftly tied a tourniquet around the leg. Max had his head turned to the side and we could see him trying desperately not to gag.

"Sorry," he said as he lifted his nose up in the air and took a deep breath, "blood makes me barf. I'm a wimp. Sometimes I even pass out."

"Oh dear, another fainter. Ginny here already passed out on me this morning. You two are sooo delicate!" Kayla teased.

I stared at Max. *Not just a pretty boy, are you Max?* As much as I wanted to hate Max for taking my Owen, and I really, really wanted to hate him, I just couldn't. For someone who fainted at the sight of blood, it must have been super hard to spend the morning with the guy he loved bleeding out in his lap and to never leave his side. Impressive. Nothing says love like stepping up when it's life or death. If Owen had to be with someone else, Max seemed like a strong second choice. I didn't think that I could have done the same in Max's shoes.

"You've seen the tweets and news online, Max?" Kayla tried to keep him distracted.

"No," he replied weakly. "I dropped my phone somewhere in here this morning and didn't want to move to look for it once I was with Owen. What's the latest?"

"Rumor has it that the shooter might be done and we might be getting out of here soon," I told him.

"Can't be soon enough," Max said sadly.

"Well I think Owen owes you big time after today, Max," Kayla tried to lighten the mood. "Definitely more than splitting dinner and a movie. You make sure he foots the bill."

"The only reward I need is for O to be okay," Max said.

I didn't know what to say. I was struck by how old and tired Max sounded. Maybe we had all aged in the hours since the shooter had arrived and ripped our lives apart. It seemed like an eternity since Mom had dragged me out of bed and I had been nasty to her, dismissing her worries about my cutting and stalking off. Had that really just been hours ago? It seemed like another lifetime. Wait until I told her about Owen, she wouldn't believe it. Or maybe she had already guessed? Mom and I hadn't really talked much lately. I'd been shutting her out, staying in my room more, hiding my cuts from her again. Why had I been such a bitch to her this morning when she was clearly just worried about me? It was just the two of us now, and she was probably outside panicking that she could lose me today too. Kayla tapped me on the shoulder, bringing my pity party to a close.

"I'm just going to check on Miss Jones. You comin'?" she asked.

"Sure," I said.

We crawled back to Miss Jones. The green mound that was her covered corpse was now surrounded by objects. Origami swans and notes written on paper hearts:

RIP Miss Jones
Never forgotten SWHS 2019
Gone too soon
We will meet again
Love you Miss Jones XO

There were even bracelets and crosses that students had taken off and placed beside her.

"This is so messed up," I said to Kayla. "Why did this happen? Why us? Why here? Why today? It's so random and impossible."

"I can't answer that, Ginny," Kayla said. "It makes no sense to me either. Don't get sucked into those thoughts now. I've seen the news coverage of school shootings in the States, but I never really paid attention. Never once did I think for the tiniest fraction of a second that it would ever happen here. But we just have to keep it together a little while longer. You can do this, I know you can."

I was fed up, and furious, and sad, and confused, all at the same time. I wasn't so sure that I could keep it together anymore. I entertained the thought of going batshit crazy and throwing a desk through a window and climbing out to safety. Or being the hero and opening the door and just walking out into the hallway and out the front doors. *You want a piece of me, well here I am.* I'd either end up a hero or dead. I didn't really want to be either. I just wanted to go home.

National News
@news4you

#BREAKINGNEWS: Evacuating @SouthwesternHS students in view, hands in air. Emotions running high as families reunite. Confirmed reports of casualties #education #breakingnews #nationalnews #schoolviolence #gunviolence #wearefollowing #staytuned #SouthwesternStrong

1:40 PM–April 28, 2019. Ottawa ON
♡ 894 ⟲ 2.1K ♡ 2.2K

Chapter 20

As **more text** messages were exchanged and tweets read, and the news feeds started to pick up on what was unfolding at Southwestern High, the students around me were starting to panic. It was becoming clear from social media that some students had exited the school, either escaped or been rescued. I overheard that most news feeds were also reporting that the shooter was "neutralized." The whir of helicopters overhead was unmistakable; I guessed they were either medic choppers airlifting the injured or news choppers angling for a closer view. The red and blue lights flashing through the slats in the blinds on the windows had also grown more intense as more teams had arrived outside.

"What the hell?!" Jace could be heard above the quiet chatter.

"They've forgotten us!" someone called out, their voice shaking and frantic.

"What do you think?" I whispered to Kayla. "Think we were forgotten in the madness?"

"No way," she replied. "I'm sure these things just take time. But it can't be too soon for Owen I don't think."

"Or Miss Jones," I said.

"I just hope that no one does anything stupid now that the end is in sight. I read about a kid getting shot once because he was fleeing from danger somewhere and the police mistook him for the gunman," she said.

"Do you think they took out the shooter?" I asked. "If they did, I hope no one else got caught in the crossfire."

"Me too. I'm guessing that they either took him out, or arrested him, or he killed himself. They seem to do that when the police close in."

My friend Daisy's dad was a cop. I remember Daisy telling me that he would go into her room at night when he came home after a shift and wake her up to kiss her goodnight. She insisted he do that so she would know he got home safely. He had a safe hanging on the wall in the basement of their house where he kept his gun. Whenever we had to go in Daisy's basement to get our scooters or to get a soda from her snack fridge, I would leave extra space to walk around the safe like it could reach out and get me. The safe was locked tight with a huge padlock and a combination lock, but I was terrified of what was inside. I had been raised with a healthy fear of guns, and Daisy and I had been told repeatedly that the safe was off limits. I didn't even want my arm to brush against it, that's how terrified I was of what lurked inside.

Now that it felt like any imminent danger might have passed, I was willing to sit tight in Homeroom A as long as necessary to avoid any crossfire or any interactions with the shooter. But others weren't so patient. They wanted fresh air, and food and water, and to escape from the stench of the tiny bathroom that was now wafting into our bloody sweaty Monday prison.

"Paul just told me that he is being bussed to the hospital to get checked over with a bunch of other students," she said. "He said he's not sure whether the shooter is still in here."

"Is he okay?" I asked her.

"Yes, he's fine. He's a big guy with the heart of a teddy bear. I'm sure he took care of whoever was trapped with him."

"Sounds like you two will make a perfect couple," I said trying not to sound jealous.

"You will have to meet him," she said. "I know you would like him."

"Sure," I said.

"He's going to college for vet school next year. His family has a farm with horses and pigs and goats. I know he's birthed a few of the horses even," Kayla bragged.

"Great," I lied. "You too can get cowboy hats and a big old truck with horns on the front and live happily ever after."

"What's that supposed to mean, Ginny?" she asked.

"Whatever you want it to mean, Kayla."

She looked at me with a hurt, puzzled expression, unsure why I was lashing out.

"After today we will all go our separate ways." I tried to explain. "We're stuck with each other right now, but we won't be once we get out. You and Paul will move on, and Max and Owen will too."

"Why, Ginny! Is this your way of showing me you care? Your twisted messed-up way?" she asked.

"I don't know," I admitted. "But today is *Twilight Zone* and tomorrow everything will be back to the way it was. Maybe I'm just not sure what that means for me. Never mind."

"No, I get it. *This*," she said waving her hands to indicate the chaos that was Homeroom A, "is exceptional. Not normal. And it'll be hard to figure out how to deal with it and how to go back to real life. And how to even feel safe again."

"Yeah, I guess," I agreed. "Maybe it's only just starting to sink in for me. I've been on autopilot all morning."

"Well, let this sink in to that thick skull," she poked me in the forehead. "Whatever *this* is," she waved her good arm around again, "we've dealt with it together, and we will walk out of here together. And a bond like that doesn't just disappear, cute vet waiting in the wings or not. You're stuck with me now, Ginny Bartholomew. Besties."

"Good to know, Barbie," I said only half-joking. I let out the breath I'd been holding in. Besties sounded pretty nice.

Southwestern Mayor's Office
@REALSWMAYOR

Call 1-800-555-9945 to check on status of loved ones. Please use 911 for EMERGENCIES ONLY Resources limited today #SouthwesternStrong #loveoneanother

1:55 PM–April 28, 2019. Southwestern ON
♡ 945   ⤺ 2.3K   ♡ 2.9K

Kayla and I jumped, startled, when someone started banging on the classroom door. The force of the bangs weren't as hard as before, the windows weren't rattling this time. Still, it was frightening and very unexpected.

"Anyone in there?" a deep male voice called out. A new voice. No one made a sound.

"You can open the door. It's safe now," the voice said. "It's SWPD."

Kayla stood up and walked over towards the door but stopped about 2 feet away. She was vulnerable now, a target. And fearless.

"I am not opening this door for you," she said loudly. "We haven't been given an all clear."

"The all clear was given. Please open the door so we can help you."

This time Kayla didn't respond. The room stayed quiet and she walked over to the left side of the door and slid down the wall to sit on the floor. She pulled out her phone and started to text. I crawled over and sat down beside her. I wasn't fearless.

"Good call," I said. "We can't open it up until we know who is on the other side. Who are you texting?"

"My mom." She continued to type. "Mom is going to find someone to ask if we should open the door, she knows our room number."

We waited, hoping Kayla's mom would find out quickly. We were so close to the end.

"Anything?" I asked anxiously a few seconds later.

"No, Ginny." She was staring up at the ceiling, lost in her own thoughts.

C'mon, c'mon, c'mon. My patience was shot. I needed out of there.

No one else in the room spoke or moved. No one was crying or whimpering anymore. All were on pins and needles wondering how this day would finally play out. They had all relied on Kayla and me a few times today and now their safety lay completely in Kayla's hands. They obviously trusted her. And no one was stepping up offering to be the one to stand in front of the door in her place either. Go figure.

"Here goes," Kayla said, starting to type again. "Mom says they texted Miss Jones a few times to tell her the SWPD was coming to let us out."

"Well that explains it," I said. "I'm not going over there to check Miss Jones for her phone though. No way."

"It's fine," Kayla said. "They've given us a code word to ask for. If he says the same word that the cops gave to my mom, then we can move the blind on the door and verify that it's someone named Officer Snegg on the other side."

Kayla took a deep breath, stood up again and reclaimed her spot a few feet in front of the door.

"Okay," she demanded, "If you are SWPD, what's the code word they gave me?"

"Miss Jones," the officer called back.

Kayla visibly buckled, her hand went to her mouth and she let out a sob before she could stop herself. She then straightened back up, stood a little taller and walked over to the glass. Kayla lifted the blind a few inches and peered out. I scooted around to try to get a glimpse of who was out there. The person on the other side had a helmet on with a tinted face guard and I could see the top of what must have been his tactical vest. His gloved hand was pressing his ID badge against the window. The badge read *Officer Snegg SWPD.*

Kayla called out, "I can't see your face."

Damn Kayla, you are handling this like a boss. There was no way anyone else in the room could have stood there so calmly and called out a cop who just as easily could be the shooter ready to take her down. The cop took off his glove, reached up and slid his face guard onto the top of his head. A friendly face with a small sad smile looked back at Kayla.

"It's okay, sweetheart," he said. "You can open the door. It's over."

I couldn't imagine what she must be thinking and feeling. She stood perfectly still staring down at the door handle for what seemed like an eternity.

"Open the door, sweetheart. You are safe now," the officer repeated. "We can't help you out here."

Kayla didn't move a muscle. She was made of stone except for the slight tremor I could see in her hands. The only sign of fear.

"It's alright, Kayla. You did it. We are safe. Open the door," I tried to rouse her.

She looked over at me like she was surprised to see me and had forgotten where she was, then ever so slowly she reached over, slid the bolt back to red, turned the handle and opened the door.

After that it was a blur of voices and bodies. More officers rushed into the room and the last one shut the door behind him. A few officers zoomed straight in on Miss Jones's green table-cloth under the window ledge and ran to her. I heard Max call out desperately, "Over here, over here!"

I stayed where I was for a second, letting it all sink in. Then I stood up and went to the nearest officer who was handing out what looked like giant sheets of tin foil and wrapping them around people.

"What should I do?" I said. "Do I run?"

"Sit tight, hun," he replied. "We are all leaving here together."

Officer Snegg announced that we would all follow him out of the room and walk down the hallway to the side entrance. We would then walk out with our hands in the air, cross the tarmac and continue on to the church parking lot across the street. There were tents set up there with food and drinks, and our families were waiting for us. He said that most of us would then be put on buses to go to the hospital and get checked over. His team had brought in stretchers and they were handing out bottles of Gatorade.

"Alright," he announced loudly. "Please follow me, arms in the air and we will all head outside. We will be taking Owen out first and then Miss Jones. If you are able, please help those around you who can't help themselves."

Out of the corner of my eye I saw Jace rush over to the officer and speak to him. Officer Snegg nodded. Jace, Gregg, Steve and a few other guys assembled around Miss Jones, lifted her stretcher and made their way to the door. They waited for the stretcher carrying Owen to clear the door, then they followed the officer out into the hallway, then we all filed in behind. No one jockeyed for position, no pushing or shoving. I started to follow too, my hands in the air, when Kayla came up beside me and pulled one down to clutch in hers.

"Remember what I said, Ginny? You and I are destined to be besties. We're leaving here hand in hand."

"I do," I said. "Thank you, but maybe we should lift them up just for our own safety," I chuckled. "For you, maybe just the one. The good one."

"I guess you're right, sure would suck to get shot now," she laughed.

"Nice symbolism though Barbie, I like that. Great in a movie," I deadpanned.

The hallway was dark, no lights on, just the glowing exit signs and dim backup generator lighting. The smell of gunpowder assaulted my nose. I tried to keep my gaze high and not look around, but I saw the blood outside our door. Owen's blood? The shooter's? Tables, chairs and garbage bins were strewn about. Some of the windows had bullet holes in them and shattered glass. When we passed through the final outer door the sunlight was blinding. My eyes burned. I couldn't see anything for a few seconds and the world stopped.

Despite the crowds of people, and the incessant sirens, and vehicles and equipment that I knew were everywhere, all was silent for me. I was walking in a vacuum except for the sound of the leaves rustling in the birch trees beside the school. No other sound. I followed the others, making our way like some macabre parade, hands in the air, foil blankets fastened at our necks, reflecting the white sunlight. We must have looked like shell-shocked aliens in silver capes. We reached the parking lot and started to scatter as loved ones appeared to claim us. I saw her right away. Mom was running towards me full speed, arms waving out in front. I didn't know what she was saying, but I kept walking in her direction. I took my last step towards her, unfastened the foil blanket and dissolved into Mom's arms. She caught me before I collapsed to the ground. The volume returned to my world and I could hear an anguished voice wailing, "I love you" over and over. The voice was mine.

Southwestern Mayor's Office
@REALSWMAYOR

Candlelight vigil planned in Grand Park this evening 9pm All welcome #SouthwesternStrong #loveoneanother

3:05 PM–April 28, 2019. Southwestern ON
♡ 877 ↻ 1.6K ♡ 1.3K

Chapter 22

All was a blur. A flurry of movement. EMTs, police, nurses, doctors, all scurrying around, barking orders. Asking questions, carrying stretchers.

"IV over her now!"

"There's more coming out, be ready people."

"Live from KWES news ..."

"My son, where's my son?!"

"You are safe now, we've got you."

"Dad!"

"Our Father who art in heaven ..."

"Stay back, please! Behind the tape!"

Voices. Sirens. Screams of agony. Wailing. Tears of relief. I couldn't concentrate. My ears were ringing and I was getting a migraine. Where was Kayla? When did we let go of each other's hands? Was that Mrs. Turner? Miss Jones? No, couldn't be her. Where was Owen? Max? MJ?

I was outside. I drank the Gatorade and I ate the banana that was placed in my hand. People were in my face, their eyes huge. Asking me questions, I think. But their voices were like Charlie Brown voices, making no sense.

I was in the back of an ambulance. Legs dangling off a stretcher. Mom's arms were around me, not letting go. A pressure cuff was on my left arm. A thermometer, in my mouth.

I had secured a classroom from a madman shooter.
I had calmed classmates in shock.
I had stitched up human flesh.
I had watched my teacher die.
I had watched Owen get shot.
But I was free.
And I was tired.
So very, very tired.

Prom Night

"**O**ne more pick-up, then it's paaartaaay time," Paul cheered from the back of the limo.

Owen's mom had booked the huge SUV for the six of us so that no one had to drive. She would also be hosting an after-prom party for about forty of us later on in the evening. Owen's mom was a highly regarded wedding planner, so I had a feeling it would be off the charts. I couldn't wait.

Owen seemed to be healing as well as could be expected. His stitches were out, and he and Max were too. Owen was finally able to walk without crutches, with just a slight limp, a souvenir of that horrible Monday. He'd been going to therapy, both physical and mental, for the three months since the shooting. He was assured he would make a full recovery, physically at least.

He and Max looked amazing sitting on the side bench in the limo, hair slicked back, wearing jet black tuxes with black polka dot bow ties and yellow kicks — a stunning couple very much in love. Kayla and Paul didn't look too shabby either, and appeared just as you'd expect the wholesome boy and girl next door to. Kayla's off the shoulder tulle confection of a dress was yellow as well, a hopeful, happy color. The tiny scar on her shoulder was a faint reminder of what she'd been through. Paul's bow tie matched his cornflower blue eyes, and I had to admit, he was pretty hot. Nicest couple you'd ever meet, but tough as nails when their friends needed them.

There was talk in town of leveling Southwestern High School and building new somewhere else, making the school's footprint a memorial to the twelve people who had died that day. Some citizens felt that was giving in to the shooter, some wanted to rebuild on site. For now, the school remained as it was, a crime scene. We had never returned to class after that Monday. The year had ended early. I had no idea what would happen in September for our final senior year.

I was seeing a therapist, working through what I experienced in lockdown. I had a hard time with sudden loud noises and confined spaces. I skipped the Victoria Day fireworks and spent the evening in my room reading a book, noise canceling headphones on tight.

If I thought Mom was over protective before the shooting, she was now out of control. She wanted to know where I was at all times, when I'd be home, who I was with. She bought me the latest iPhone and I swear if she could place a tracker in my ear like they do to dogs, she would.

I was trying to ease myself off the cutting, but it was a hard habit to break when I felt broken. Sometimes when I cut, and the blood bubbled up, the smell and sight of it sent me right back to that morning in Homeroom A. Sometimes I wanted to be back in that moment, to try and make sense of what happened and feel that bond and trust that we had all shared. Other times I didn't want to even acknowledge that it had happened.

But when I was struggling and felt like no one else could understand what I was feeling, I called Owen, or Kayla, or Max, or MJ, and we would talk for hours. They got it. We'd always have that day in common. Like the identical tattoos we all shared with the date of the shooting inked on our wrists, *APRIL 28 2019 RIP*.

"Here we are," Kayla hollered over to me. "Think your date is ready?"

"I sure hope so Prom Queen Barbie, cuz this girl wants to dance!"

I smoothed the skirt of my purple organza gown, silently rehearsing what I would say when my date appeared. I wanted to nail it.

The driver got out and came around to the side door and opened it, ushering my date into the back with the five of us.

"*Buenas* nachos *hermosa dama*," I addressed MJ as she awkwardly tried to navigate the high step up in her stilettos. Her periwinkle beaded strapless dress shimmered in the late afternoon sun.

"Um ... thank you, I think," she replied. "But I'm pretty sure it's *noches*, not nachos," she said, a huge grin spreading across her face. "Good try though, Ginny! And by the way, you all look amazing." MJ looked relaxed and confident. She was not the same person who had shown up for class in Homeroom A that sad Monday. None of us were. I had crossed numbers 1,2,3,4 and 6 off of my to-do list, but mastering Spanish was going to take longer than I thought.

The month before, when Kayla found out that she would be getting one of the many student awards for bravery from that awful day, and that she and I would be celebrated as Prom Queen and Queen for our "exceptional leadership and compassion" in extreme circumstances, she insisted that the six of us go together as a group. She was embarrassed by the accolades and the fuss in the press, but we wouldn't let her get out of it. Kayla deserved every bit of recognition and every reward.

Not everyone was going to the prom, some were no longer with us, and some just weren't ready to have fun and maybe never would be. But we were ready to party and celebrate the fact that we were breathing and together. Who knew what the next Monday would bring? Or the next week, or the next year?

Whatever the future held for us, we were going to *carpe* the hell out of every *diem*.

Acknowledgements:

For my parents, always and forever.

For my mentor, Lou Duggan, who made me trust my wings and not the branches.

For my baby girl, Bronwyn, who gave up her sleep on the long drive to and from the island to talk about Ginny. Any time I spend with you is a gift.

For my son, Dylan, who keeps me current and still answers my rambling texts. I am so proud of the man you have become.

For Marisa and Emily, who saw that first rough draft and treated me with kid gloves, and for Angela and Jenna, without you there is no Boot Snack!

Thank you to "The Herd", Kirsten, Emily, and Ellie, for believing in my story and taking it to that next level.

Most importantly, this book would not exist without Bruce (especially the tweets!), my BF, my safety net, my travel buddy, and my biggest cheerleader. You are one of a kind, you save me every day, you listen to my writing over and over and over and over and always have something to offer to make it better.

And finally to Lucy, for keeping my feet warm while I type and only asking for a carrot and a butt scratch in return.